A Spot of Grace

ANJ
Press

Pittsburgh

A SPOT OF GRACE
ANJ Press, First edition. March 2026.

Written by Amelia Addler.

Cover design by Lori Jackson
https://www.lorijacksondesign.com/

Maps by MistyBeee

for the moms

Recap and Introduction to

A Spot of Grace

Our Spotted Cottage story began when Sheila moved to San Juan Island following her divorce. Her goal was to rescue her (now ex) mother-in-law Patty's tea shop and home from her ex-husband's greed. Not only did she succeed in that, she also managed to capture the heart of next-door neighbor and movie star Russell Westwood.

Sheila and Russell also struck up a scheme to help free Lottie the orca, who had been captured by Sheila's dad from the waters surrounding the island decades prior.

The island's charm and magic slowly but surely pulled in Sheila's daughters Eliza and Mackenzie, Russell's daughter Mia, and Sheila's sister Addy. Each of them discovered a peace within themselves on the island – and fell in love.

The newest resident to retreat to the island is Annie Thompson, childhood friend of Jacob Kowalski (son of Hank Kowalski of *Saltwater Cove* fame).

With Jacob's encouragement, Annie made the tough decision to separate and divorce her husband Roy. Now, with her twin toddlers, Annie is trying to piece her life back together.

It's not without its challenges, especially living on an island. Roy made a permanent move to Seattle, and Annie is left questioning if she should follow him to make things easier for her family.

Except, despite the difficulties living on an island brings, there is also a community that refuses to let her struggle. Her mom, Clara, welcomes her into her home. Patty and Sheila insist on helping, and as always, Margie won't allow anyone to suffer on her watch.

Plus, there is a distractingly handsome firefighter down the street who no one can take their eyes off of, Annie included...

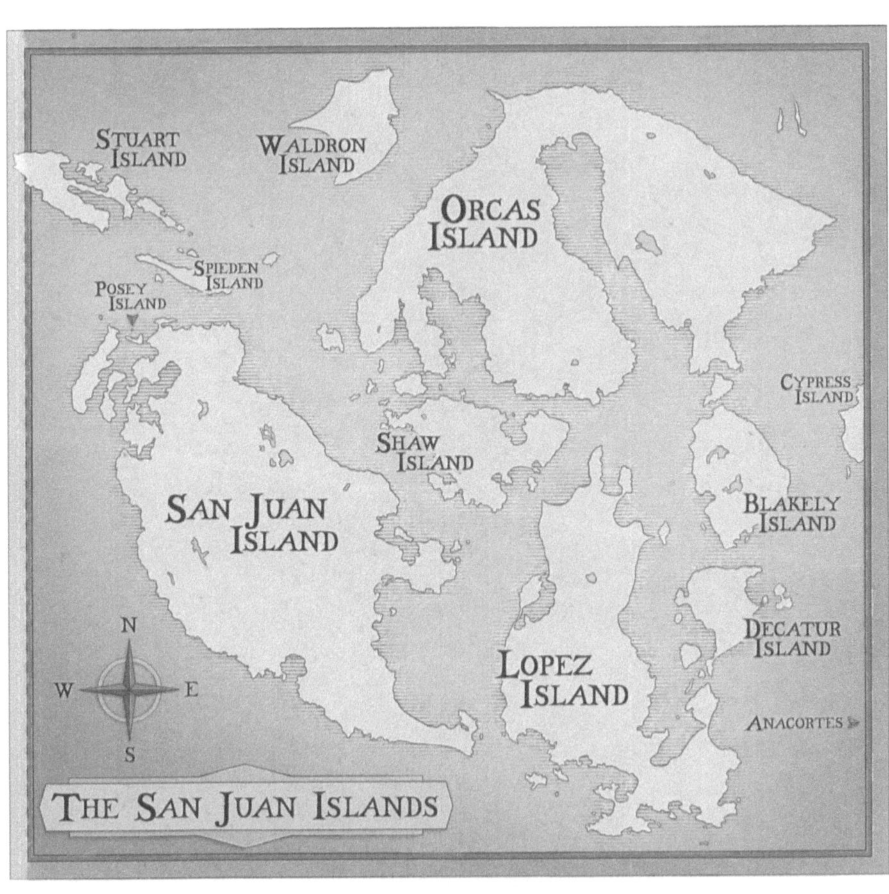

STUART ISLAND
WALDRON ISLAND
ORCAS ISLAND
SPIEDEN ISLAND
POSEY ISLAND
CYPRESS ISLAND
SHAW ISLAND
SAN JUAN ISLAND
BLAKELY ISLAND
DECATUR ISLAND
LOPEZ ISLAND
ANACORTES
N
W E
S
THE SAN JUAN ISLANDS

One

Annie stood knee-deep in the waters of Westcott Bay, fifty degree water pressing against her waders.

She stayed focused. So focused that she almost missed the vibration of her watch — her 3:30 alarm, telling her it was time to stop work or risk being late for picking up her twins, Noel and Leon, from daycare.

With an eight o'clock drop off, it didn't leave much time for work, especially on a day she was in the field—like today. She'd nearly finished gathering the oysters to test for the *Vibrio parahaemolyticus* bacteria, but another half hour would get her everything she needed...

It wasn't worth being late, though. Annie stopped, casting her eyes toward the shoreline and wiping her hand on the inside of her jacket.

Fall on San Juan Island was beautiful, like every other season. Evergreens rose to the sky, standing out against the gray drizzle, and swathes of red- and yellow-leafed trees dotted the landscape.

When she and Roy had moved here during her pregnancy, he said it was the most beautiful place on earth. He used to say *she* was the most beautiful woman on earth.

Not beautiful enough, apparently, to keep him from becoming her ex-husband.

Annie waded out of the sea, the damp air chilling her skin, and walked back to the lab outpost.

Inside, she stripped off her waders and changed into the clothes she'd worn into work that day.

Annie paused to look at herself in the mirror. Her hair was wet, strands clinging to her forehead, but otherwise there were no signs she'd been at work. Scientist Annie was gone, replaced by Mom Annie. Her grey shirt was at least five years old, pilling at the seams, and her jeans pinched at the sides.

These were pre-pregnancy jeans, and despite the twins being nearly two-and-a-half years old, she refused to buy new ones. It was a matter of practicality. Jeans were expensive, and she'd have to go to the mainland to try on new styles. There was no time for such luxuries.

Plus, she had her pride. She'd fit into these jeans again without her love handles spilling over... one day.

She said a quick goodbye to her coworkers, then made the short drive to daycare and rushed inside.

Her dear friend Jacob had done pickups for a while, but when he and his girlfriend Mia got the chance to work in Vancouver, Annie insisted he take it.

"They don't need me in Vancouver," he'd said. "I'm needed here."

"You're *appreciated* here," Annie said, "But I'm not going to hold you back. I'm fine!"

And she'd meant it. They had an amazing opportunity and were newly in love. Annie loved having him back on the island – they'd been close friends since high school – but she could handle things on her own.

Plus, Annie's mom Clara was planning to retire and become her new helper. How much help did she need?

"Unfortunately," Annie told him, grinning, "you've been made redundant."

Jacob laughed. "I can't compete with such an experienced candidate."

"You really can't."

At first, it all went swimmingly. Her mom loved spending time with the kids, and after Annie had to sell her portion of the house in the divorce, she had moved into her mom's small two-bedroom house with the kids.

She told herself it was only temporary, until she could get back on her feet. Her mom insisted it was better that way. Cozier. And for a while, it seemed true.

Then her mom fell while hiking and broke her hip, and Annie was back to the reality of drowning in laundry, dishes, and night wake-ups, while also trying to advocate for her mom.

"Hi!" Annie said, spotting the daycare teacher as she walked into the room. "How are you?"

She gave a small smile. "Doing well. How are you?"

"Good! Did Leon's speech therapist come in today?"

"Yes," she said softly, stepping closer.

Something in her facial expression made Annie's stomach sink.

Annie leaned in, voice hushed. "Did it not go well?"

"Leon had a tough day. We had an incident." She pulled a sheet of paper from Leon's cubby and handed it to Annie. "Leon hit another student."

Annie winced. At home, they talked about not hitting. They read books about not hitting, practiced taking deep breaths, and talked about what he could do instead of hitting.

Yet Leon, red-faced and fury-fisted, kept hitting, and he didn't have the words to tell her why. Since her mom had disappeared to the rehab facility, he'd stopped speaking entirely.

"I am so sorry," Annie said.

The teacher cut her off. "It's okay. Something to be aware of. Something we're working on. Leon had difficulty engaging with the speech therapist today. Next time will be better."

Did her optimism come from years of experience, or was she offering an empty kindness? Annie swallowed the thought behind a stiff nod.

Leon caught her eye from across the room, and a grin spread across his face.

Annie smiled back. "Yes. Next time will be better."

She grabbed their backpacks, took Noel's left hand and Leon's right, and led them out to the car.

They made great time to the grocery store, and Annie managed to get them into the shopping cart without protest, pleased that her snack cup offering had satisfied them both.

Maybe things weren't perfect, but she could hack it. She wasn't going to lose her cool during this blitz-shopping trip.

She was going to get them home, make dinner, feed everyone, then pack them into the car to get dinner to her mom, too.

A bit ambitious, but Annie was going to do it. Annie was going to do it all.

She pushed the cart into the store. No time to waste. Leon looked around, wide-eyed and chewing, and Noel sang, "I'm a cup, I'm a cup!" over and over – her rendition of *I'm a Little Teacup*.

Annie reached into her pocket for the grocery list she'd put together on her lunch break.

Nothing but crumbs.

She searched her other pockets, then her purse.

Empty.

Annie shut her eyes. What good was a list if she'd forgotten it?

She tried to remember what she'd written from her new cookbook with the perfect combination of affordable, fast recipes that her twins might eat and with enough leftovers for her mom to enjoy at the rehab facility.

The ingredients refused to surface in her mind. Annie opened her eyes.

It was fine. She wasn't going to lose it over a silly list. She had a vague memory of what was required, and all at once, she realized the recipe might be on the author's blog.

She started a search on her phone, and as it was loading, a word floated into her mind.

Enchilada sauce! That was it, the oddball ingredient.

She was standing right in front of them, as though her subconscious had guided her here. She stooped down, eyeing the prices for the cheapest one.

"Well, if it isn't my favorite set of twins!"

Annie looked up, swiveling her head to see who had interrupted her thoughts. An older lady stood above her, beaming at the twins.

She recognized her from church but couldn't remember her name on the four hours of broken sleep she'd gotten last night.

"Hi, how are you?" Annie said brightly, standing up.

A drop of sweat slipped down her back. Maybe she needed a snack, too. Her hands were shaking ever so slightly.

The woman waved at the twins. Noel smiled and waved back. "We buy cookies," Noel said with a nod.

Cookies were *not* on the list.

The woman leaned in, her face inches from Leon's. "Cookies are good, aren't they?"

Leon turned to Annie, his lips pressed into a firm frown. He was not a fan of strangers. Or of being asked questions.

"Oh yes, they both love cookies," Annie said, sweeping him into her arms before the tears erupted.

The cheap sauce would do. She grabbed it and threw it into the cart, then pulled her phone from her back pocket.

The recipe had loaded. Thank goodness. Beans, and a can of crushed tomatoes with chiles. She never would've remembered that.

The woman let out a tsk. "You need to let him speak for himself or he'll never find his voice."

A crimson heat crept onto Annie's neck. Her eyes flicked up at the woman, then back down at the recipe.

Two pounds of chicken thighs. Totally forgot that, too.

"Mhm," Annie said, as evenly as she could, before pushing the cart off and away.

Leon, recovering with the offending woman was out of sight, wiggled out of Annie's grasp and got his feet onto the ground.

There was no use fighting him back into the cart. They only needed a few things.

"You have to hold my hand," Annie said, straining to push the cart with one arm. Her wrist cracked in protest.

No time to slow down. She pushed onward, using her body weight to keep the cart from going sideways into a display.

She rushed, throwing things into the cart, and due to a momentary lapse in judgement, Annie let go of Leon's hand in the dairy section. He made a beeline for a display of cookies, toddler legs pounding furiously away.

"No!" Annie cried out, lunging to grab him.

It was too late. The small round table crashed to the ground, plastic clam shells of cookies exploding open and cascading across the floor.

Her mouth dropped open. "I am so sorry," she said to no one in particular.

"It's only a few boxes," a man's voice responded. "I've got it."

Annie was already on the floor, trying to gather the cookies up with one hand while holding onto Leon's arm with the other. Leon was undeterred, trying to shove a cookie into his mouth.

"Ginger snap," the man's voice said. "No one will miss them."

Annie glanced at him and her heart sank. All she could see was a head of thick dark hair, and a pair of broad shoulders. He was working steadily, his movements far less frantic than Annie's.

He looked up at her, his brown eyes framed with impossibly dark lashes, a sympathetic smile on his lips. Her heart leapt and she forced her gaze down back to the crumbs in her hand.

Was it her low blood sugar, or was she dizzy from looking at him? Maybe it was the act of being down on the ground.

Annie shot up to her feet. She couldn't crawl around on the ground for so long. Noel could fall out of the shopping cart.

Thankfully, she hadn't done so yet. She'd just watched the scene with her mouth open.

Leon had taken one bite of the cookie and thrown it to the ground. Annie stooped to pick it up just as an employee arrived with a broom and dustpan.

"I'm really sorry," she said, cheeks burning.

"It's okay," the woman said with a shrug.

The beautiful man was standing again, towering over them both. "Does that mean I get these at a discount?" he joked.

The woman let out a loud laugh and Annie retreated with her cart before the beautiful man could say anything to her.

Talking was not in her wheelhouse today.

In the safety of the aisle, she regained a bit of her composure, grabbed the last two things she needed, then made her way to checkout.

Annie was relieved to see it was their regular cashier, a middle-aged lady who always gave stickers to the kids.

Leon insisted on helping unload the cart. He produced a container of chocolate chip cookies first, and as Annie tried to piece together when he'd snuck them onto the bottom of the cart, he helpfully threw a dozen eggs onto the conveyer belt.

Miraculously, the eggs didn't break.

"I, uh, made a mess in the bakery," Annie confessed. "I can pay for whatever I spilled – "

The cashier waved a hand. "Don't worry about it. One of those days, huh?"

Annie nodded, hands shaking as she bagged the groceries. The rushing, the low blood sugar, and the beautiful stranger were threatening to send her over the edge.

But she wasn't going to lose her cool. Even when the total came out $26 over budget.

She would have to take a look at the receipt at home. They couldn't go over budget every week.

Outside, the drizzling rain had finally stopped, leaving an overcast sky. She got the kids into their car seats first, then handed a cookie to each of them.

A voice floated into her ear. "Well, didn't you make a mess in there."

Annie's back stiffened. She turned.

The old woman who had almost made Leon cry stood like a statue in powder blue slacks. Gold chains encircled her neck and arms, as she stood, slowly shaking her white-coiffed head.

If Annie's blood sugar wasn't cratering, she would have thought of something clever to say.

But she'd had a salad for lunch, then two coffees, and she could hear Noel screaming inside the car.

So she narrowed her eyes and said, "I'd like to see you prove it."

Annie returned her cart, got into her car, and after making sure no one was looking, stuffed an entire cookie into her mouth before driving away.

<h1 style="text-align:center">Two</h1>

Margie Clifton stood at the edge of the grocery store parking lot, her arm high in the air, waving wildly.

Annie was inside her car, her hand in front of her mouth. She paid no notice to Margie's show as she drove off.

Margie's arm dropped to her side. Had Annie been crying? Had she been sobbing into her hand?

It sure looked like it. What was going on?

She could call Annie – or no, better call Clara. She reached for her phone, but before she could make the call, a voice interrupted her.

"Young people are so rude these days. Always looking at their phones, never taking the time to talk to anyone around them."

Was this person calling her young? Margie was going to be fifty-five after Christmas. It had to be someone trying to flatter her. Or –

Margie turned and sucked in a breath. It was Deborah Wills, an odious woman who forced Margie to practice her patience.

"Phones are useful, after all," Margie said with a smile.

Deborah scoffed. "Are they? I think they're turning everyone into robots. That's why I don't have one."

"Ah."

"I just ran into Annie Thompson," Deborah continued, "You know, with the twin babies?"

Margie knew her well. Her stepson, Jacob, had been close friends with her growing up on the island. He'd just moved away, but they'd spent many a happy evening all together at Margie's house.

Surely Deborah must know Annie was dealing with a runaway ex-husband who had abandoned her with two young children?

Deborah lowered her voice. "You know her son can't speak? May be why the father left. You never know."

Margie's patience snapped like a rubber band. "My own husband left me for a younger woman. Awful when men make those sorts of choices, isn't it?"

Deborah blinked at her. "Yes, it is."

"Terrible to judge others, Deb. You should think on that." Taking a few steps forward, Margie smiled. "Have a blessed day!"

She walked off without looking back.

The nerve of that woman. Had she said something to Annie to make her cry? If she had, then she deserved far ruder treatment than either Margie or Annie could muster up.

Inside the store, Margie grabbed a cart and called Clara.

Thankfully, she answered right away. "Hi, Margie."

"Hi, Clara! How are you? I'm sorry I've been absent recently. Things have been so busy with weddings and parties."

When Margie had moved to the island years ago, she'd converted an old barn into an event venue – Saltwater Cove. Her pride and joy, since her children had all flown the nest.

"Oh, that's all right. I've been keeping busy. I guess Annie told you?"

"Told me what?" Margie asked.

"About my fall. I didn't want anyone to know, but I guess it's time. It happened about two months ago. I broke my hip," she said with a groan.

Margie stopped abruptly and the shopping cart behind her slammed into her legs. She sucked in a breath, steadying her voice. "No!"

The woman with the offending shopping cart rushed around to mouth a "Sorry!" and Margie smiled and mouthed back, "It's okay!"

"Yeah," Clara said. "I'm in rehab now, slowly getting better."

"When will you get to go home?"

"That's the thing," she said with a sigh. "I might be able to go home next week, but I'll need some things installed and I don't know who can do it on such short notice."

"What do you need?" Margie asked.

Clara sighed. "Embarrassing things. My mom always said not drinking my milk would catch up to me, but – ugh. Now I need grab bars in the bathroom, a handrail for the stairs I never got around to installing, a handheld shower head. Little things."

"I'll find someone," Margie said with a nod.

Her husband Hank could probably do it, but he might need to take some time off work. As the Chief Deputy Sheriff, that wasn't always possible...

"No, you don't have to do that," Clara said. "This is why I didn't want anyone to know what happened."

"Please," Margie said. "It's my pleasure." She gasped. "Annie. She's been all alone, hasn't she?"

"I was hoping she'd reach out to you for help but... now I realize how naïve that was."

Ah. That could explain the tears. Annie only accepted help when it was forced on her, and even then, reluctantly. "I'll be over tonight."

．　．　．

Within three hours she finished shopping, made an enormous baked ziti, and arrived at Annie's doorstep.

Margie knocked. The door didn't swing open for a full two minutes, but when it did, there was chaos.

"I come bearing gifts," Margie said with a smile.

Annie's face fell. "My mom called you, didn't she?"

"Not exactly." Margie stepped inside.

Toys were strewn across the floor. She could hear the twins squealing in the next room. Three baskets of laundry sat next to the couch. Margie couldn't tell if they were clean or dirty.

"I saw you at the grocery store today," Margie confessed.

Annie groaned. "Another witness."

"You were crying," Margie said softly. "It's okay to – "

Annie cut her off. "What? I wasn't crying."

Margie paused. "In your car? When you were leaving?"

A distant look formed on Annie's face. "No." She slowly shook her head. "No, I was stuffing a cookie into my mouth."

Margie laughed, clapping a hand to her mouth. "Oh! Well, I called your mom and found out your secret."

"What's my secret?" Annie asked. "That I'm hopeless at doing anything on my own?"

"Oh hush. Is that why you're so against asking for help?"

"What about the state of my home makes you think I need help?" Annie asked with a wry smile.

Margie wasn't there to judge. She had three grown children. She knew how these things went. She was also old enough to know how silly it was to be ashamed of it.

Margie carefully stepped over the toys and made her way to the kitchen. The sink was overflowing with pots and pans. "I heard your mom was in the hospital, and you're all alone."

"Plenty of mothers are able to take care of their children on their own," Annie said, adding a soft, "except me."

There it was. Margie dropped the pan on the counter and pulled Annie in for a tight hug. "Is that what this is about? You are taking care of two little kids by yourself. You're doing great. Where are they, by the way?"

Annie broke the hug. "They're in their cribs. They just had their baths and should be going to sleep."

Noel sang out, "Jingle Bells!" as if on cue.

Annie sighed. "I wanted to get dinner to my mom before they had to go to bed, but I ran out of time."

"I'm happy to watch them if you want to run and see her."
Her eyes cast down.

"What?" Margie asked. "Do you really think my home looked any different when I had little kids and my husband was off on business trips all the time?"

"You're always put together, Margie."

"Ha! Hardly! I'm just in a different stage now. My mom was over helping *all* the time. And one of my cousins who had kids slightly older than mine came over a lot, too. But it was still chaos."

Annie was quiet for a moment.

"I know you don't like asking for help…" Margie continued.

"I don't like asking for help all the time," Annie corrected. "You'd think a few days here or there and I'd be able to right the ship. It makes me feel…" Her voice trailed off.

Margie smiled at her. "I know, but the demands are endless, and you're only one person."

Annie nodded. She picked up the baby monitor. "Wow. Did you cast a spell on the house? It looks like they both might be asleep."

"Perfect! They won't even know I'm here. What do you want to do? Go to bed? See your mom? Have a night on the town?"

A weak smile crossed Annie's face. Her eyes were so tired. "I'd like to go see my mom. I made chicken enchilada soup for her."

"Then you go and see your mom," Margie said, pushing her toward the door. "I'll stay as long as you like."

"Are you sure?"

She took Annie's coat off its hook and guided her arms into it. "Positive. Go. Relax. Listen to silence on the drive over."

"Thank you, Margie," Annie said.

Once she was out the door, Margie got to work. First, she tackled the kitchen – putting away clean dishes, washing the pile in and around the sink, and wiping down surfaces, including the crusty microwave.

Then, she tidied the toys, folded the laundry, found a pike of dirty clothes and got it into the dryer before Annie got back.

"Any issues?" Annie asked as she rushed in the door.

"None at all."

She dropped her purse with a sigh. "It looks great in here. Thank you, Margie."

"It's my pleasure. What else can I do?"

Annie put her hands up. "Please, you've done enough. More than enough. You should go home."

"I don't mind spending the night so you can catch up."

"Don't be ridiculous. But thank you, Margie. I really appreciate it."

"I know you do." Margie grabbed her coat and squeezed Annie's hand. "I know how hard it can be. I'll be back tomorrow!"

"No – " Annie started, but Margie only smiled and disappeared out the door.

Three

"That's enough!" Annie yelled.

Leon and Noel froze. Noel was halfway to the other side of the ferry, and Leon had one leg up on a table.

Whenever she had to take them on the ferry, Annie always foolishly imagined driving on board with them sleeping peacefully in their car seats.

But there was no sleeping. There was no keeping them in their car seats. Annie's only option was to take them upstairs, onto the passenger decks, where they ran amok as she chased after them, her face red and her nerves pulled as tight as violin strings.

Their excitement over the boat, and the water, and the people, had built to an explosive crescendo until someone ended up yelling – normally, all three of them. This time, Annie broke first.

As per tradition, she immediately felt terrible, but it was too late. The mood was ruined, and as soon as she got control of them, the announcement rang out that they were pulling into Anacortes ferry terminal.

She'd almost made it the entire way without losing it.

Almost.

She took each twin by the hand and rushed them back to the car. Noel was defiant, whining, and Leon was sullen. Annie drove off the ferry and straight to their meeting place with Roy, the local McDonald's.

He was already waiting when she got there, arms crossed over his chest as he leaned against the hood of his new Mercedes.

"Was the boat late?" he asked.

No *hello*. No *how are you*. Only Roy's new car and his ever-tightening t-shirts, his muscles larger and more veiny than she'd ever seen them in their nearly two decades together. Was he trying to get down to zero percent body fat? Every time she saw him, it gave her a jump scare to see him looking so wiry.

It looked like Roy, but it wasn't Roy. It wasn't the man she'd loved for so long. It was his uncanny mid-life crisis replacement.

"It was late, yeah." Annie pulled open Noel's door.

She was mindful not to apologize. It wasn't her fault the ferry was late. The ferry was always late.

"Hi girlie!" he said brightly.

"Daddy!" Noel yelled, arms outstretched.

He pulled her from the car seat. "This wouldn't be a problem if you'd move to Seattle like you said you would," he murmured, a bright smile on his face.

Heat rose in her head, flaring as it hit the top.

Annie took a deep breath. She was not going to lose her temper again in front of the kids, and she was not going to make this exchange any worse than it needed to be.

There was no need to point out that if *he* hadn't moved from the island it wouldn't be a problem, that his job was remote and he didn't need to live in the city in the first place, and that it was far too expensive for her to live in Seattle, especially since she'd had to drop out of her PhD program during their divorce and now she was stuck earning the same wage she'd earned while she supported him through his career growth.

She wasn't going to say any of that *out loud,* at least.

"Did you remember the extra clothes this time?" he asked.

She unbuckled Leon. "I did."

Noel whined, unhappy no one was listening to her, and threw her hands to her face in anguish. "Time for snack!"

Annie clenched her jaw. Of course. The kids were not only tired; they were hungry. They'd missed their nap for this exchange, and despite their excitement over the ferry ride, they were tense, too.

And what had Annie done? Instead of anticipating this, instead of reminding herself of these facts so she could be the adult in the situation, she had yelled at them.

The situation was hard to get used to for everyone. Initially, during the divorce proceedings, things were so civil it didn't seem they needed a formal custody agreement. Roy was adamant he'd be seeing the kids fifty percent of the time.

The idea of being away from them so often broke Annie's heart, but she said nothing. She knew the kids needed their dad.

In practice, however, it ended up being more like one week-end a month, or whenever Roy could coordinate his work schedule, and his hiking schedule, and his mom's schedule.

They'd also left out any formal child support negotiations, because Roy reasoned they would both have the kids half the time and didn't need it.

Annie could kick herself now, but at the time, she was dealing with her high school sweetheart. How could that man be the same one who could hardly find time to see his kids? One whose monetary support dwindled to nothing, lest Annie nag and beg him for it?

Which she wouldn't do.

"I already had to buy another set of car seats," he added, taking Leon by the hand. Then, more loudly, "Hey buddy, how's it going?"

Leon stared at him.

Annie opened her trunk, her hand scraping on an edge of rust. She wiped her hand on her pants. "Here is the diaper bag and their extra clothes. I packed some snacks for the car. They did not have a nap on the ferry."

"Terrific," he said sarcastically, flashing a fake smile.

Annie helped get them into the car, and once the doors shut, she stood back and waved.

"I'll see you soon. I love you."

This time, Annie managed to bite the tears back until she got into her car. Roy pulled away, the car disappearing from sight in seconds.

This was the moment she'd imagined all week—watching them drive off. Her nerves were shot, and all morning, instead of enjoying her time with them, she'd rushed around and worried and run from that image.

Now, she sat in the silence. There were no tiny voices whining. No hands reaching for her.

Wasn't this what she wanted? A break? Wasn't this what she'd wished for only a few days ago, when they were within reach? They'd all three sat at the dinner table, yogurt smeared everywhere, all giggles and screams.

But no, now there was nothing but guilt. Annie took a breath and got out of her parking spot.

There was some time before her return trip to the island. She made the drive out of town to a restaurant she'd always liked and ate a meal by herself at the diner counter. She forced herself to read a book on her phone and sipped on coffee.

She managed to get through five chapters, more than she'd gotten through all month. The daring Viscount risked it all and now there was no doubt how he felt. He was the perfect man, playfully flirtatious but astoundingly noble. Handsome. Fiercely in love with the woman of his dreams.

A fantasy, she knew, but one she couldn't look away from.

On the drive back to the ferry, a billboard caught her eye. She blinked twice, thinking she was imagining it. It was a picture of a man – a firefighter – in a white shirt and yellow suspenders. He had black hair and smoldering brown eyes. It almost looked like the man she'd seen at the grocery store – but no. It couldn't be.

Beneath him read, "Marry my dad! Email Bella226@eemail.com and tell me about why I should pick you!"

Annie sputtered out a laugh. It couldn't possibly be real. She wanted to take a picture, but she couldn't react in time.

Luckily for Annie, there were more ads on the ferry. One, where the handsome stranger had an ax slung over his shoulder, took up the entire wall near the bathroom. It said, "He didn't start the fire! My dad is looking for love, contact me to see if you're a *match!*"

It *was* him. The unbelievably handsome cookie rescuer. She stared at him, unashamed because he wasn't able to look back at her.

No wonder she'd gone into shock when she'd seen him. He was the most beautiful man she'd ever seen.

Annie chortled a laugh and snapped a picture, immediately sending it to her mom. It was just the sort of thing that would cheer her up, sitting alone in that rehab facility.

She replied right away. "That is too cute! Should I submit your resume?"

"Ha ha. Don't even think about it," Annie texted.

"How was drop off?" her mom asked.

"Not bad," Annie lied.

Her mom sent back a sad face. "Try to take your mind off things. Do something fun this weekend. Something other than coming to see little old me."

Well, *that* wasn't going to happen. Though her mom insisted she was making friends, Annie didn't buy it. She felt awful she wasn't able to come and see her more.

On the bright side, Margie said she'd find someone to help get the house in order so her mom could come home soon. That would help her breathe easier.

Four

Light sparked on the water, the sun making its morning appearance draped in purples and blues. Miles glided on the surface, the lean muscles of his arms causing hardly a ripple. It was so cold all he could focus on was his next move, a meditative rhythm of left, kick, right, kick.

He turned his head to sputter out a chilled breath before grabbing onto the ladder at the dock. Miles stood, steam rising from his skin, as he towel-dried in the morning air.

It felt good to be back to his daily swims. His buddy let him use the dock, and it was much easier getting out here in the morning now that Bella was back in school. All summer, they'd stayed up binge-watching TV shows into the late morning hours together. He had hardly made it out a dozen times.

He, of course, mourned the fact that they had to cut back on their tradition, but he had to put on a brave face for her. She struggled enough with getting up in the morning for high school – she didn't need to know he was one more "Please?" away from giving in to another episode of *Parks and Rec*.

The rest of fall was a celebration—the changing leaves, the crisp air, the return of some calm to the islands as the tourists made their way back home.

He cast one more glance at the foliage before disappearing into the boat house, getting dressed, and jogging to his car. The skin on his arms was still numb; normally, he'd do push-ups to warm himself back up, but he had things to do, like make Bella's new favorite breakfast – two egg whites, chopped green pepper and mushrooms, and a slice of whole grain toast with butter and strawberry jelly.

He needed to pick up a jar of jelly from his friends' farm. They kept a stand of goods by the road, and payment was on the honor system. He took a short detour, got the jelly, and made it home in time to make breakfast for them both.

Bella made her way downstairs ten minutes before she had to catch the bus.

"Happy Monday," he said, sliding her omelet onto a plate.

She took a seat at the kitchen table, peering up at him. "Happy Monday."

"Are you feeling okay?" he asked, taking a seat next to her. "I can make you something else if you're not feeling an omelet."

"No, this is good. Thanks, Dad."

He wasn't going to push. She always came to talk to him eventually – or at least, she *used* to.

At fourteen, it seemed she was pushing him further and further away, to the edges of her life. He knew teenagers needed to reject their parents to find their own identities (or so the books said), but why *his* daughter? Couldn't they be the exception?

She'd been his world from the moment she came into the world. She was his best friend – not his confidant, he knew that was too much pressure for a kid – but she was his everything. And he'd always been hers, too.

Maybe that was over now. Was it the gradual beginning of the rest of their lives, where she was too mature and cool to confide in her old dad? Or was it, mercifully, just a phase?

His chest tightened at the thought, and he forced down the rest of his coffee with a gulp.

She made it to the bus on time, and after cleaning up, Miles got in his truck and drove to the fire station.

He'd been a full-time firefighter just over six years. Bella used to think it was the coolest thing in the world. "My daddy saves people," she'd tell her friends, or people in the grocery line, or attendants on the ferry. Never a shy child, she loved to say what was on her mind.

What did she think now? His bubbly little girl had turned into a quiet, brooding teenager. Half the time, he couldn't tell if she was sullen or thoughtful. Maybe she was both.

Inside the fire station, the mood seemed off from the moment he walked in. Everyone was looking at him with half smiles on their faces.

"What's up? Is there something on my shirt?" Miles asked.

They scrambled, leaving his buddy Sam to face him.

Sam shook his head. "Nope, nothing on your shirt. I was wondering if you found any matches recently."

Miles tilted his head. "What matches?"

"You know," shrugged Sam. "To start a fire."

He frowned. "Are you talking arson?"

Clarissa, one of the part-timers, popped her head into the room. "Not to start a fire, Sam. Just a match."

Miles sat in his chair and leaned back. "Are you all on something?"

Clarissa laughed. "So...you haven't seen it yet."

"Seen what?" asked Miles.

She put her hands up. "I'm not going to tell him," she yelled, disappearing into the kitchen.

Sam let out a heavy sigh. "I guess it falls on me."

Miles wasn't going to play Sam's game, whatever it was. He turned without a word and logged onto his computer.

Sam appeared at his side, crouching low, phone in his hand. "We all heard you're looking for a *match*," he said.

Miles sighed. "Sam – " He glanced over, doing a double take at Sam's phone. It was a picture from the fundraiser he'd been bamboozled into doing months ago.

A firefighter calendar. What a terrible idea it had been. Miles had felt like a show dog, propped up with an axe, told to hang off a ladder. It was awful.

He'd only agreed to do it because they badly needed to raise money to repair a fire engine that had been out of commission for months. Sam had argued Miles was the only one who could contribute. "No one's going to pay to see my beer gut," Sam had argued.

It was in conjunction with a few other firehouses, and the pictures were never supposed to make it back to San Juan

Island. They'd promised the calendars would stay on the mainland. It had been months; he thought he was safe.

"Is this a joke, Sam?" Miles asked.

Sam chuckled, first quietly, then the laughter overpowered him. He coughed, clapping Miles on the back as he doubled over.

When he recovered he said, "I swear to you, it isn't. This was on the morning ferry yesterday."

Miles stood from his chair. "Clarissa," he bellowed.

She didn't come out of the kitchen this time. "It wasn't me!"

He went back to Sam's phone and looked more closely. There was text under his picture.

"Help my dad make a match," Miles murmured. He sighed. "Bella."

"I gotta admit," Sam said, "she's topped any prank I could ever pull on you."

There was an email listed—Bella's.

He turned back to his computer and typed out a message. "The jig is up. Expect a talk. - Dad."

.   .   .

That afternoon, he decided to pick her up from school. When she spotted him sitting in the truck, her face broke into a grin and she ran over.

"You finally figured it out," she said.

"What do you mean, finally? How long have these things been up?"

She shrugged.

He turned to look at her. He'd expected her to be remorseful. Apologetic. Not whatever this was. "Bella, have you lost your mind? Do I need to explain how disrespectful this is, putting my picture up for strangers, and how dangerous it could be?"

"It's not dangerous at all," she said with an eye roll. "You kept asking me what I wanted for my birthday this year, and this is it."

He felt eyes on him. Bella's three best friends peered from the schoolyard, giggling when he looked.

He sighed and pulled out of his parking spot. "I'm not having this discussion. We're getting everything taken down. Where did you even get the money for this? This had to be expensive."

"It wasn't. I won it."

"You *won* it?"

"I thought you'd be proud! I'm taking a marketing and communications class, and I had the most impressive ad campaign, so I got offered a two-week deal to advertise whatever I wanted."

A smile began on her lips, then she laughed, holding her stomach, laughing and laughing.

Miles clenched his jaw. "Bella."

She wiped away tears. "It was supposed to be ads for the school play, but I swapped the images out at the last minute. I can't believe it worked."

"This isn't – what you did – it's not funny," he said finally.

"Oh, it's not meant to be funny."

He knew he was guilty of not disciplining her enough. For the most part, he hadn't needed to. She was a great kid, and they had excellent communication and understanding.

She was his favorite person in the world, but maybe it was a mistake to not be more stern. At least on occasion.

Now might be such an occasion. "Until you understand how serious this is and how wrong it is, you're grounded."

"Grounded? What does that even mean?"

"It means that you're in trouble. You can't go out with your friends —"

"What! For how long?" she shrieked. "That's not fair!"

"What's unfair is you putting up pictures of me like cattle for sale!"

"Well, how else are you going to find a wife if you don't get out there?"

This again. Last year, she'd decided he needed to start dating again. Then it escalated to him needing to get married.

He'd thought she just wanted to plan a wedding and wear a pretty dress, so he had taken her out to a fundraising event and thought that'd be the end of it.

"I'm not looking for a wife," he said. "I don't know what got this into your head, but this isn't how things are done. And you can't force me into anything – this is my life, Bella."

"It's *my* life too. I've never had a mom, and maybe I want one!"

"You have a mom," he said, much louder than intended.

She was quiet, arms crossed over her chest. "Not a living one."

His jaw clenched. Ever since becoming a teenager, she'd found a way to make words sting like never before.

"I've always given you everything you needed," he said, regaining control of his volume.

"Except for a mom," she snapped.

A weight sunk in his chest. "What's wrong with it being you and me?"

She sighed and rolled her eyes. "You're not even listening to me. You *never* listen."

That was so far from the truth he couldn't think of a response. He pulled up to the house and as soon as he had stopped the car, Bella got out and ran, slamming the front door behind her.

Miles shook his head, muttering a request to his late wife. "Give me the patience to survive this, Madeline."

Five

After a rainy weekend, October gifted them a beautiful week – dark blue skies painted with clouds so blindingly white Margie could barely withstand their glare.

The air was crisp and perfect, the wind cutting through her still damp hair as she hurried into the tea shop.

"Sorry I'm late," Margie called out as she walked in, the door jingling to announce her arrival.

Warmth engulfed her, along with the smell of bergamot and cinnamon. The tea shop was quiet, save for a table of teenage girls sitting in the Japanese-themed room.

"I just got back from Annie's," Margie added as she pulled off her coat.

"You're never late," Patty said, emerging from the kitchen with an apron tied around her waist and a three-tiered stand of treats in her hands. Apple turnovers, cucumber finger sandwiches, and some assortment of cookie bites. Delightful.

The long-time proprietor of the tea shop, Patty wasn't showing any signs of slowing down in her eighth decade of life. It helped, of course, that her daughter-in-law Sheila had moved to the island to help a few years prior. Sheila liked to joke that she'd made out like the devil in her divorce – she got to keep the house *and* she got to keep her mother-in-law.

"What were you doing at Annie's?" Sheila asked.

She sat at a nearby table, pouring tea from a beautiful pink-and-gold teapot.

Margie took a seat next to her, her cheeks flushed pink from rushing. "Leon spiked a fever at daycare and she asked if I could pick him up."

"Oh!" Sheila handed Margie a cup of tea. "I'm surprised she asked for help. I wish she'd ask me for help! I love those babies."

"Don't be offended. She only asked me because she was on a boat in the middle of the ocean for work and couldn't make it back quickly enough," Margie said, taking a sip. Paris tea with a hint of lemon. Her new favorite. "Annie is still Annie. Trying to do it all on her own."

Patty took a seat, a frown etched on her face. "Poor Annie. That husband of hers..." She narrowed her eyes.

"She's better off without him," Sheila said, cutting her off. "If he doesn't want to be around, let him leave. One day, those kids will grow up and he'll be full of regret."

Patty turned to her, a smile dancing on her lips. "Are you speaking from experience? About my son, perhaps?"

"Perhaps," Sheila said.

"I don't care about him." Margie waved a hand. "I care about Annie and the twins. Clara is supposed to come home from the rehab facility next week, and she needs some modifications to the house so she can get around safely. I went over to take a look, and I thought Hank could do it, but he threw his back out. He was laid up all weekend. I need to find someone else."

"Russell won't be back in town until two weeks from now," Sheila said. "Maybe we can do it ourselves."

Margie sighed. "We can, but it won't be pretty. My skills lie elsewhere."

"Mine too," Patty said, placing a cookie bite on each of their plates. "Try these – my new pumpkin spice cookie bites."

Margie lifted the little orange cookie to her lips and took a bite. The outside was crisp, with warm cinnamon and hints of ginger. Inside was a rich, soft buttery center.

"Is that cream cheese?" Sheila asked.

Patty nodded. "What do you think?"

"It's marvelous," Sheila said, adding another cookie to her plate.

Margie finished her cookie and took a sip of tea. "Really perfect, Patty."

One of the girls stood and walked to their table, a smile on her face. "Hi Margie!"

"Oh, hi Bella! I didn't see you over there. How are you? How is your dad?"

"We're good," she said slowly, "I didn't mean to eavesdrop, but I think I heard you all talking about babies?"

Margie nodded. "You heard right."

"Well, I was going to talk to you anyway, but this is perfect timing. My friends and I want to start a babysitters club on the island."

Sheila's eyes lit up. "That is such a good idea."

"Thank you!" Bella turned to her, beaming. "The only problem is that some of us don't have much experience with kids. Or, you know, any experience."

"I see," Margie said. "That does make it more complicated."

"Since you know everyone on the island, maybe you'd know someone who would be willing to teach us? In particular, teach me?"

Margie laughed, "Of course! I know a few people who could use a mother's helper. Actually, I have the perfect mom who lives just down the street from you. Do you know Annie Thompson?"

"I don't. Do you think she'd be opposed to me having no experience?"

A smile took hold of Margie's face. This was perfect – in fact, it might be the only way to get Annie to accept any help. If she felt like *she* was helping someone...

"I think she'd be quite happy to have you, but I'll have to check." Margie gasped. "I bet your dad could help fix up some things around the house for Annie's mom, too!"

"I'm sure he'd be happy to!" Bella said, grinning. "He's always doing that sort of stuff."

"Maybe this weekend we can all get together? I'll talk to your dad."

"Great!" Bella clapped her hands and squealed. "Thank you, Margie!"

She went back to her table of excited voices.

"Perfect cookies, perfect day," Margie said, pouring tea into her cup.

"Is her dad *the* island firefighter?" Sheila asked, leaning in. "You know, the one in the dating ads?"

Patty chuckled. "He is."

"Miles? Dating?" Margie shook her head. "There's no way."

"You haven't seen them?" Patty asked.

"I have no idea what you're talking about," Margie said.

Sheila slid her phone across the table. On it was an image of Miles carrying a ladder over his shoulder with the words, "On my way to rescue your heart."

A gasp escaped from Margie. "What on earth?"

"He didn't make them. Allegedly, Bella did it," Patty said, "She got them posted all over the ferries."

"Ah. That makes more sense," Margie said.

Miles was handsome, brave, and a wonderful father. To Margie, it seemed like he was just begging to be set up. She'd tried, years ago, to play matchmaker with the island's most eligible firefighter. It went quite poorly.

"Even *I* know that Miles Coleman is unmatchable," Margie said. "But I admire Bella's fighting spirit."

Sheila sat back, eyes wide. "I never thought I'd see the day where Margie Clifton gave up on trying to set someone up."

"A nut too hard to crack?" Patty asked.

"He is an uncrackable nut," Margie said with a nod. "I thought I was being subtle, trying to set him up with one of my daughter's friends. Do you know he came to my house after and gave me a firm—but polite—talking to? He would not be subjected to my romantic hand, he said. I thought I would die of embarrassment."

The three of them burst into laughter.

"He told you, didn't he?" Patty said.

"He did!" Margie shook her head.

A smile crept onto Sheila's face. "But you're going to send him over to Annie's? With no underlying intention?"

"No," Margie said firmly. "I'm not going down that road again."

Patty caught her eye and smiled. Margie bit her lip.

She believed what she'd said.

Mostly.

Six

"Thank you so much for doing this," Lauren said, climbing into the passenger seat.

Annie smiled at her. "It's my pleasure. I'm sure when my car inevitably breaks down, you'll get to return the favor."

Lauren's head flashed back in a cackling laugh. "You crack me up. Don't say that. Don't jinx your car into being like mine."

Annie didn't think it was *that* funny, but she appreciated the laugh. Lauren was like that. She smiled easily, laughed easily—she just seemed happy.

Did Annie seem happy? *Was* she happy?

Happiness was what everyone wanted, but so much of the time she felt overwhelmed and guilty and over-wrung, like a towel with every last drop squeezed out.

She didn't want to be this way. How could she be more like Lauren? Lauren, with *four* children, was always laughing and had perfect hair and stylish clothes and was so, so kind.

Maybe it was experience. Her youngest was in the same class as Leon and Noel, which was where Annie had met her. She'd already raised three kids past this age. That had to count for something, right?

They'd done a few playdates at Lauren's house. Leon loved her son, and Annie loved going over there.

Lauren's older kids were sweet and polite. Her eldest daughter always wanted to play with Noel, and she was so gentle and creative. Lauren's husband was sweet and attentive, insisting on making lunch and firing up the grill. He was a real family man, the kind of guy Annie thought Roy would be once they had kids.

Instead, for whatever reason, Roy had cracked into pieces and ran off.

Annie shook her head and snapped herself out of it. She didn't want to stoke any jealousy about her friend.

"Do they think they'll have it fixed for good?" Annie asked.

This was the third time Annie had given Lauren a ride to pick up the car from the mechanic. It seemed whenever one issue was fixed, another cropped up.

Lauren waved a hand. "Who knows? Every time they promise me it will be the last visit. At what point do I stop putting money into this car?" She rolled her eyes. "We just can't afford a new one right now."

"I hear you on that."

Annie wasn't jealous of Lauren in a spiteful way. If anything, Annie admired her. Desperately admired her.

She wanted to be like her, more carefree, more even-tempered, more spontaneous. She wanted to be the fun mom.

"My parents offered to loan me one of their cars, but they don't understand what irreversible damage four children will do to the interior," Lauren said with a laugh. "Perry's parents only have the one car – you know, their minimalist lifestyle, which I totally get. But wouldn't it be nice if they had an extra minivan lying around?"

Annie smiled. "Did you ever think you'd hear yourself saying those words?"

"Never!" Lauren leaned forward and turned up the dial on the radio. "I *love* this song!"

Annie hadn't even noticed there was music. She was still thinking about how involved all four grandparents were in Lauren's life. Every time Annie visited, there was at least one set of grandparents present, if not both.

That had to take a lot of the load off. To have people around, always available to make food or wipe faces or babysit.

Annie couldn't even coordinate a time to get her hair cut. Her mom had been helping before her fall, but she felt guilty enough about that. Now, she had no one.

The haircut would have to wait. She'd considered taking scissors to the annoyingly long locks herself, but she knew she'd look deranged.

There was so much joy in Lauren's house. Bickering, of course, but that was family. What kind of family would Noel and Leon end up with?

Her heart constricted in her chest. She had to remind herself that even if she had stayed with Roy, his plan was to keep an apartment on the mainland and use the island as his "home base." There was no promise that he'd even be around...

Her mom would be back soon. She was days away from discharge. Margie promised she had a guy to help prepare the house for her arrival. Annie had no idea how she would pay him, but she would figure something out.

They arrived at the car shop and Annie pulled into the lot.

"Thanks so much, girl." Lauren said, opening the door. "Do you want to come over with the twins next weekend? I'm going to do a little Halloween thing. Pumpkin painting, cookie decorating."

"Sure! They'll love it."

Annie would love it too. It made her feel more normal to be around other families with kids, even if it meant falling behind on the never-ending dishes and laundry.

"Great. Just show up whenever on Saturday. I'll see you later."

"Good luck with the car!"

Lauren made a face and rolled her eyes.

Annie laughed to herself, then made the drive to daycare to pick up Noel and Leon.

They were both in chipper moods, having just gotten over a thankfully mild case of hand, foot, and mouth disease.

Annie got the worst of it, starting with a wicked cold and now a cough that wouldn't go away. At least her fingernails hadn't fallen off again...

Yet.

This year was still better than the last, as far as illnesses went. During their first year of daycare, the twins were sick so severely and so often that Annie had felt like daycare was nothing more than a virus library – they'd go one day, then be home for a week with whatever they'd picked up.

"Aunt Margie is going to come over later," she told them once she had them in their car seats.

Noel clapped her hands and Leon grinned, happily munching on cheese puffs.

When they got home, she set them up in the living room with toys and some fresh fruit. Though they wanted to come with her and tug at her legs, the baby gates kept them contained.

Annie had kept the gates between the living room and the rest of the house, but they'd have to go once her mom came home as to not cause another fall. It felt like the last thing she needed was two toddlers and all their toys underfoot...

A knock rang out at the front door. Annie rushed over and pulled it open to see Margie.

"Hello there!" Margie called out, waving at the twins.

They both looked up and smiled, then returned to fighting over a puzzle.

"Hi Margie," Annie said, then looking past her, gasped.

Behind Margie stood a gorgeous, dark-haired firefighter – *the* firefighter from the dating ads. And the grocery store. And her dreams.

He was too handsome for this world, a brooding, smoldering-eyed hunk of a man cut from muscle and fire.

Despite herself, she blurted out, "It's you."

"Excuse me?" His brow furrowed.

"I'm so sorry, I've seen you before. On the ferry. On an ad on the ferry," she said slowly.

A polite smile formed on his face. Or maybe it was a pained smile. "That was my daughter's doing. We are no longer accepting applications."

Margie laughed. "I dare say you were never accepting applications."

"No, I was not."

"Annie, this is Miles Coleman. Miles, this is Annie Thompson, Clara's daughter."

"Hello," he said with a nod.

"Hi." Annie swallowed. He clearly was not amused by her, and though she recognized him, he clearly didn't recognize her. She wasn't going to remind him about the grocery store cookie incident.

"I thought it was quite genius," Margie said, stooping down to plant a kiss on top of Leon's head, then Noel's. "I admire her entrepreneurial spirit."

Miles shook his head. "I'd prefer you didn't tell her that."

Margie laughed, completely nonplussed by his annoyance. "That was what I wanted to talk to you about, Annie. Miles' daughter, Bella, is starting a babysitters club."

"How nice," Annie said, hiding her face by picking up toys as the redness dissipated. "If she needs any guinea pigs, we're available."

"That's *exactly* what I was hoping you'd say. Bella and Miles live just down the street, and Bella approached me because although she wants to start this babysitter's club, she doesn't have any experience with children. I think she feels a little insecure about it."

"That's so sweet," Annie said. "I loved babysitting when I was a kid."

"Would you be willing to take her on as a mother's helper, perhaps, to teach her some of the basics?"

Annie's chest filled with air and a smile forced its way onto her face. "I would love that. It would be my honor."

Margie clapped her hands together. "Wonderful. I'll tell her to come over while Miles starts on some of the work. Do you have a list of what needs to be done?"

"I do," Annie said, reaching into her pocket. "This is what my mom's physical therapist recommended. It's a lot. Maybe we can just do the basics."

Miles accepted the list, his eyes scanning.

Margie went on. "I brought dinner. Another baked ziti! It's enough for everyone."

"It's one of the twins' favorites." Annie smiled and glanced at Miles. He was carefully looking over her list, brow furrowed. Or he was ignoring her.

"You need a handrail for outside?" Miles asked, looking up at her.

"Yes," she said.

He didn't seem annoyed, just serious. Maybe she'd misread him. She'd be sure not to do anything else annoying.

"I'm not sure which one to buy or how much it'll cost," she added.

He waved a hand. "We've got a fund for that sort of thing at the fire station."

"Really?" Annie felt a weight off her chest. "I'm happy to pay you for your time, too."

Miles shook his head. "No need. Consider me an extension of the fire department. We're happy to help the community."

Annie smiled. "Thank you. I really, really appreciate it."

Now wasn't that something? She didn't have four grandparents, but she had Margie. And she was part of this community.

Helping Bella start her babysitters club would be something, too. She could finally feel like she was contributing instead of taking.

Annie took the pan from Margie's hands. "I'll get this into the oven."

"Then you can show me some of these other areas that need changes," Miles said.

"Sure."

Margie was already down on the floor playing with the twins.

Annie took a breath. It was going to be okay. Her mom would come home, and the house would be safe for her. They wouldn't have to move out.

Then she could try her hand at being a happy mom, too.

Seven

Another billboard chaser, and this one right down the road. Bella's email had been flooded with them. Hundreds of emails.

How, Miles had no idea. The ads were only up for a week and a half. Maybe it ended up online somehow, because despite taking everything down, they were still getting emails with pictures and pitches with long, sad stories. Bella was particularly enchanted by a pediatrician who lived in Seattle – or at least, that's who she claimed to be.

"There's no way to tell if these women are telling the truth," Miles told Bella. She'd spent the entirety of dinner one night reading him email after email and showing him pictures.

"Why can't you just find out for yourself?" Bella argued.

"Because, as I told you," he said, keeping his voice steady, "It's not fair for me to lead someone on, especially if they're as nice as you say they are."

Somehow, this satisfied her. Or maybe she thought she just needed to find the right person.

That was more likely.

And now, this neighbor. Annie. She'd gaped at him like he was a celebrity. It was embarrassing.

Had she concocted this whole thing to throw her hat in the ring?

No, that seemed unlikely. The request for help had come from Margie, so it was most likely legitimate. Or at least, he hoped it was.

"You'll stay for dinner, right, Miles?" asked Margie.

It was best not to get too friendly regardless.

"It depends what Bella is up to this evening," he said.

"She's on her way over," Margie said matter-of-factly. "She already said she'd stay."

Oh well. "Sure, why not? I'm going to get started on this list."

Annie popped out of the kitchen, then led him down the hallway, talking over the list she'd made for her mom's return.

It wasn't much, but Annie's tone sounded as though she was asking him to remodel the kitchen.

"I don't know if this is possible," she'd start. Or, "If you think you could..."

He finally had to cut her off. "It's really not a problem. This is a tiny house, and it's nice of you to let your mom live with you."

She responded with a hesitant smile. "Thank you. I appreciate it."

He hoped he hadn't insulted her, but it was too late. After all, it was a small house. Only two bedrooms, the first with two cribs jammed against a wall, and the second with a single queen bed.

Did she have to share a bed with her mom? Or did she sleep on the couch?

"I'm worried that all the toys are going to make her trip, and I'm worried about this bed, too. I don't know how she'll get out of it. It's too tall."

Miles shook his head. "This is a good height. She just needs a pull bar to steady herself."

"Oh." Annie frowned. "How does that work?"

"It slides under the mattress. It's easy, so don't worry about that one."

She took a deep breath and nodded, eyes scanning the room. "Do you think we should move the dresser out to give her more room to walk?"

He shrugged. "We can, but where would you want to put it?"

"Good point." She frowned. "Okay, now the bathroom."

It was down the hall, a cramped space with a pedestal sink, a short toilet, and an old, high-sided tub with colorful bath toys spilling out of a hanging basket.

"I can get some pull bars in here, and a shower seat," Miles said.

Annie nodded. "A shower seat, right. The physical therapist said that would be helpful."

He made notes on the supplies he needed for the rest of the house. None of this was much trouble. The biggest project was the railing on the concrete stairs leading up to the house.

"I'll go outside and measure now," he said. "Do you want to pick out the railing?"

"Whatever you have is perfect," Annie said quickly.

He nodded. Margie had already told Annie they had supplies at the fire station, as well as a fund to do these sorts of improvements.

There was no fund at the fire department for this stuff. Margie was paying for all of it. She had made Miles swear he wouldn't say a word.

"What if someone else hears about it and wants the same service?" he asked her.

Margie stared him in the eyes. "Then I will pay for theirs, too. I am not joking around here, Miles. If you let a word of this slip, it will be the end of you."

Her intensity had forced a laugh out of him. "You have my utmost discretion."

He was looking at the stairs when Bella arrived.

"Hey Dad! Are you here to supervise my first babysitting job?"

He smiled at her. "Pretend like I'm not here. Act like I'm maintenance."

She gave a curt nod. "Hurry it up, would ya?"

He laughed and she walked past him, nose high in the air.

How had she managed to get her mom's sense of humor without ever having met her?

That wasn't technically true; they'd met, of course. He just didn't like to think about the circumstances.

When he came back inside, the house smelled of garlic and butter. Was he really going to turn down a Margie meal out of stubbornness?

Of course not. Instead, he posted himself at the dining table and searched the online home improvement stores for the right sized handrail.

He had a perfect view of Annie, Bella, and the twins from where he sat, but he had to pretend he wasn't watching.

"Up until they start walking it's generally pretty easy to entertain them," Annie said.

Bella shook her head. "They're so cute, but babies scare me the most. They're so floppy and small."

"That's understandable," Annie said, "but I have a friend at daycare who has a six-month-old. Nice and sturdy, holds her head up by herself. I'm sure she'd be happy to teach you about babies."

Her eyes brightened. "Really?"

Annie pulled out her phone. "It doesn't hurt that she's the cutest baby in the world."

They both leaned in, looking at a picture on Annie's phone. Bella let out a loud, "Aww!"

Miles smiled and cast his eyes down. He really shouldn't be eavesdropping, but it was impossible.

"With two-year-olds, you've got to keep your wits about you," Annie said.

At that moment, Leon climbed onto the couch and threw himself back, falling to the ground while letting out a primal scream. The muscles in Mile's chest tensed.

Bella gasped. "I should have caught him. I'm so sorry."

Annie shook her head, gathering him in her arms and planting a kiss on his head. "Are you okay, honey?"

The crying stopped and he batted his eyes at her. She kissed him again. He got up and ran off.

"Not your fault at all. They're always doing things like that; falls happen a couple of times a day. Stay calm, and if they stop crying, you're generally good."

Bella's eyes widened. "A couple of times a day?"

Miles couldn't help it. He was staring at them, grinning. Neither noticed.

"Yeah!" Annie laughed. "It's chaos!"

He hadn't really looked at Annie before. She had kind, blue-grey eyes, her laugh reaching the corners. Wisps of brown hair escaped her ponytail and framed the soft features of her face. She had delicate, smooth skin and full, red lips. She was pretty, in a very real, no-frills sort of way.

Her hands worked quickly and gently, physically showing Bella everything: how to change a diaper, how to deal with the kicking legs of a two-year-old, how to change the shirt of a feisty toddler.

Bella dutifully followed her lead, stopping suddenly at the sound of toddler shrieks, the relief on her face palpable when Annie stepped in to guide her.

Bella was doing her best, and she was doing it well. She was lucky to have found such a kind teacher.

Maybe Miles had judged Annie too harshly. She didn't seem like a billboard chaser. She hadn't thrust any headshots at him. She hadn't told him any strange puns.

She was a woman living with her two kids and elderly mom, treating Bella with the utmost respect.

He looked up and saw Margie staring at him.

"Thanks for introducing us," Miles said. "This is exactly what Bella needed."

"It's exactly what Annie and Clara needed, too," Margie said. "Do you think you'll be able to get it all done in time?"

He nodded. "I'll make a trip to the mainland to get the handrail, but otherwise, yeah, everything else I can get locally."

"Wonderful. Now, help me set the table."

Enough time gazing at his daughter. No matter how long he stared, she kept growing up.

He stood, startled by his own rudeness. "Of course."

Eight

She couldn't have offended Miles too badly, because after taking notes on the improvements they needed, he said he'd be back the next day.

Just before they left, Leon accidentally headbutted Bella in the chin. Annie half expected to never hear from her again either, but at eight the next morning, Bella appeared on Annie's doorstep with a drink in each hand.

"I brought coffee," Bella said, a tentative smile on her face. "Margie told me moms of young kids always need coffee."

Annie grinned, accepting the cup. "Margie was right. Come on in."

The twins had been up since five. Annie was due for her second cup of coffee.

"Let me give you some money for this," Annie said, rushing to get her purse.

"No, please, it's my treat," Bella said. "I had so much fun yesterday, and I feel so lucky that you trust me with Noel and Leon."

Annie frowned. She would slip the money into Bella's purse later. If Bella even had a purse. What was it kids had these days, fanny packs?

"You are too sweet," Annie said, leading her in. "You know, I loved babysitting when I was your age."

"I got the idea from my mom's old books. She had this huge box of Babysitters Club books, and I *love* them. I made all my friends read them. Now we're determined to run a babysitters club of our own."

Annie blinked at her. "The Babysitters Club books? I loved those growing up! I can't believe kids are still reading them. That's wonderful."

"See, and they say today's youth is rotting their brains with screens. Not me," Bella said solemnly, "I am reading thirty-year-old paperbacks and getting ideas."

A laugh burst out of Annie. "Not you, indeed."

Bella impressed her more and more. She was a delightful teenager. They spent the morning wrangling the kids – playing with toys, making snacks, and even getting them outside. Bella's skill in getting a coat and shoes and hat onto an escaping two-year-old had appeared overnight.

"I watched some videos," she said with a grin after Annie complimented her.

At ten, Miles arrived with a knock at the door. Annie opened it, determined not to gape at him again.

It was no easy feat. He was dressed in a black long-sleeved shirt that clung to his muscles, and a pair of paint-splattered jeans that accentuated his long legs.

He offered her a smile when their eyes met, and the warmth of it shot an electric jolt through her body.

"Hi, Miles," she said, averting her eyes and stepping to the side.

"Hey! Don't mind me. I'll stay out of your way," he said, disappearing with a shower seat and an arm full of grab bars.

As he worked and Bella laughed with the kids in the living room, Annie was able to make lunch for everyone. Mac and cheese for the twins, one of their favorites, and chicken sandwiches and egg salad for everyone else.

The rolls were fresh, crisp on the outside and soft on the inside. Sandwiches were her usual go-to during the week for lunch, and she'd perfected a few – cranberry turkey with a honey mustard; caprese with a balsamic and olive oil drizzle; Italian sub with pepperoni.

All she had today was chicken and cheese with dijon and crispy lettuce. She wished she had something else to offer but she hadn't thought of it when grocery shopping.

Annie set a platter of sandwiches on the table, adding, "I can make something else if you aren't fond of sandwiches."

Bella already had taken a bite. "No way. This is *so* good, like a professional sub."

Annie smiled. This one, though simple, was one of her favorites—a thick slab of butter on each side of the bread, creamy muenster cheese, and pepper-roasted chicken breast. The dijon had taken her ages to find; it had the perfect amount of heat and tartness to round out the flavor.

Miles nodded in agreement. "This is excellent. Are you sure you're a scientist and not a sandwich artist?"

She laughed, peeking at him as she took a seat. "I sleep so little that I don't know what I am anymore."

His shoulders shifted with a laugh. "Fair. I get that."

She'd even had time to clean up the kitchen before sitting down. That *never* happened. She was always running around, the mess in the house reaching unfathomable levels until she tackled it in the hours between the twins falling asleep at bedtime and waking in the night for whatever the reason of the week was.

"So, Annie," Bella said, leaning forward, "we're putting the twins down for their nap next, right?"

"That's right."

Bella pulled out a notebook and opened to a page with looping pink handwriting. "I see for their age, their wake window should be no more than six hours."

Annie looked at Miles, her eyes wide. "Wake window?"

"How long they're supposed to be awake," Bella added.

Miles hid his smile behind his sandwich.

"Right. I've sort of forgotten about all those rules," Annie said. "I need to revisit them, though. Good thinking."

She'd been having issues with both kids having meltdowns at bedtime. Maybe they were too tired? She and Roy used to talk these things out together. The target moved every month they got older, shifting with teeth and introducing foods and new illnesses. It was so much harder to do by herself.

Bella went on. "If they woke up at five, they need to be asleep by..." She sighed. "They're supposed to be asleep already."

She cast a wide-eyed look at the twins, sitting happily in their dual high chairs.

Annie smiled. "I think you're on to something. The more tired they are – "

"The harder it'll be to put them to sleep!" Bella finished.

"We'll get them in their cribs quickly after they finish eating."

Bella nodded. "I think if this goes well, you should just keep me here all day. I can do bath time, and a time-appropriate bedtime, then stay through the night in case there are any night wake-ups."

A laugh escaped from Annie. She didn't know how to let Bella down gently. "Though I love having your help, I don't think you should commit to *that* much time with the twins."

Bella frowned. "Why not?"

Oh goodness, she was serious!

Thankfully, Miles spoke up. "I don't think Annie signed up to take on another child full-time."

Bella's jaw dropped. "I am not a child. I am a young woman."

"Certainly not a child," Annie interjected. "But I've already been tempted to keep you forever, and I don't need more reasons."

Bella smiled at her. "Really?"

"I can't loan you out that long," Miles added, shaking his head. "I'd miss you too much."

Annie looked at him, and he smiled that vibrant smile of his. Her heart fluttered against her chest.

Not only was he unspeakably handsome, he was also a genuine, heartfelt dad. How many dads would've taken the chance to roll their eyes and "joke" about someone taking their teenager off their hands?

Not Miles. He was so clearly enamored with his daughter; it showed with every word.

Bella, apparently unable to see how lucky she was, rolled her eyes. "What about independence, Dad?"

"Yeah, yeah," he said, grinning.

She couldn't keep staring at him. He would notice, and he'd feel uncomfortable, and then who would install the handrail for her mom?

He probably had women fawning over him all the time. Annie didn't need to be one of them.

Leon threw a handful of mac and cheese on the floor, and Noel followed with a squeal, signaling the end of the meal. Annie stood, wetting a cloth to wipe their hands.

"Okay, Bella. Are you sure you're ready?" Annie asked.

Bella leapt to her feet. "I was born ready. Or at least woke up ready this morning."

Miles and Annie laughed. He caught her eye again, his eyes brimming with fatherly pride.

"Into the lion's den, then!" Annie said.

Nine

The outdoor handrail proved trickier than expected. The cement step crumbled to pieces the first time Miles drilled into it. He was more careful with the next attempts, though, and was able to install everything the day before Annie's mom came home.

It wasn't just a big day for Annie and Clara; it was a big day for Bella, too. Annie had hired Bella for her first official babysitting job. She was going to watch the twins for an hour while Annie went to pick up her mom and bring her home from the rehab facility. Then she was to stay on for another hour so Annie could get her mom settled.

Miles wasn't sure about the whole thing. He offered to come along and be a free second set of hands, but Bella shot him down instantly.

"Do you think I can't handle it?" she said, arms crossed. "Because Annie thinks I can."

Where was all this vitriol coming from? It seemed to kick up tenfold after the first time she'd walked through those high school doors.

"Of course I think you can do it," Miles said, "I just want to be available if you need me. I'm always here if you need me."

"I know, Dad," she said, dragging out the "a" in "dad."

That was the end of the discussion. He resolved to make sure he was at home, just down the street, when Bella left for the babysitting job. That way, if anything went awry, he could rush to the rescue.

He had the day off and decided he could start the process of power washing the driveway. Instead, once outside, he stood and gazed in the direction of Annie's house. The volume on his phone was all the way up in case Bella texted him, but he kept pulling it out to check every few minutes.

What if Leon launched himself off the couch backwards again? What if one of the twins choked on something? Miles was ready to sprint down the road. He even had an EMS kit by the door.

The text never came, though, and before the first hour was up, he spotted Annie driving down the street. He waved at her and she stopped at the bottom of the driveway.

He jogged over.

"Hey!" she called out of her open window. "They let me take her home!"

Her smile was so wide and contagious he couldn't help himself. He grinned back. "Hi there!"

Clara leaned forward, waving, "Hi, Miles! Nice to meet you. Thank you so much for all you've done at the house."

"Wait until you've seen it," he said gruffly. "You might be sending me a bill for drywall repair."

She laughed and waved a hand. "At that old house? I don't think so."

She had a dainty, airy laugh, exactly like Annie's. It was uncanny to see them together, like a picture of Annie in the future.

"Have you heard anything from Bella?" he asked.

Annie shook her head. "I'm sure she's fine. I haven't gotten to tell you, but I'm so impressed with her."

He nodded, jaw tight.

She paused, eyeing him for a moment. "You're welcome to tag along with us if you'd like."

He didn't need to be asked twice. Miles pulled open the door and took a seat next to a large suitcase. "Thanks. I'd like that."

Annie started moving again. "I have sloppy joes in the crock pot for dinner."

"My favorite!" Clara added.

"You're welcome to stay."

He hadn't eaten anything since his omelet that morning. His stomach growled. "Are you sure?"

"Positive!" Annie said. "It's one of our favorites, and I always make too much."

They reached the house. Annie parked and quickly leapt out of her seat, rushing to help her mom get out of the car.

"I'm really fine, Annie. My physical therapist said I'm getting around great."

Annie took her arm. "I won't have you falling again, Mom."

Miles pulled the suitcase out and followed closely behind, watching as Clara approached the front stairs.

This was the moment of truth. Clara grabbed onto the handrail, bracing her weight.

"Hey, this is really nice," she said, turning around to smile at Miles.

"Eyes ahead!" Annie barked. "Stay focused."

Clara laughed. "All right, all right."

She slowly, but easily, made her way up. The front door creaked open and toddler screams filled their ears.

Miles bit his lip. Other screams might follow. Bella would not be happy to see him.

"Grandma's home!" Annie called out.

The twins came running over, attaching themselves to Clara's legs. Leon then threw his arms in the air.

"Up, up!" he repeated.

Clara stooped down to give him a hug. "Grandma can't pick you up yet, but I am so happy to see you."

Annie turned around, facing Miles. Her eyes were red.

His heart sunk. Something was wrong.

"Are you okay?" Miles asked in a low voice.

She gave a quick nod and brushed a finger under her eye. "Leon hasn't said a word since Mom went to the hospital. The speech therapist said he might have just missed her and..." Her voice trailed off.

A speech therapist. Miles hadn't realized Leon was having issues, or that he'd stopped speaking altogether. Come to think of it, Noel seemed to do most of the talking, but that had to be normal, right?

Annie took a deep breath and dabbed at her eye. Miles' throat tightened and, without thinking, put a hand on her shoulder and squeezed.

"She's home now," he said. "From here on, everyone can move forward."

He wasn't sure exactly how to comfort her, but it seemed to do the trick. Annie flashed a smile, nodded again, and turned to walk in the house.

He followed, hiding behind Annie and Clara.

"Welcome home!" Bella said. "We've been having a great time. First, we put on some music and had a dance party. Leon has some great moves. Then, Noel and I played pretend kitchen while Leon knocked over some towers I'd built for him."

Annie beamed. "That is wonderful."

Miles cleared his throat. "Maintenance. Just here for repairs."

Despite herself, Bella smiled when she saw him. "Dad! I told you I had it under control."

"I know. It wasn't my idea to come here. Annie invited me to dinner."

"It's true," Annie said. "I saw him out on the road, wandering around and looking lost."

Bella shook her head. "He tends to do that."

Annie led her mom through the house, showing her the improvements Miles had made. The excited "oohs" and "ahhs" made him feel bad.

He had hardly done anything, but they were acting like he had built a new house for them. It was a shame he couldn't build a new house for them; they sorely needed more space.

Clara returned to the living room and lowered herself onto the couch. "Miles, would you mind opening a window? It's stuffy in here."

Miles obliged, turning to pry open a large window by the couch. It resisted his efforts.

"Does this always stick like this?" he asked.

Annie appeared at his side, throwing an elbow into the frame. It popped open.

"I think something's broken," she said with a shrug.

Miles frowned. "I could fix it."

She peered up at him with those calm blue grey eyes. "That's very kind, but I think you've done enough."

"I like having things to fix." He cleared his throat. "I noticed your showerhead was also hanging down. I could replace it. While I'm in there, I can fix the bathroom vent. It doesn't seem like it's connected to the outside."

Clara sighed. "There are a lot of little things I haven't been able to fix over the years."

He paused. He'd thought this was Annie's house, but maybe it was the other way around.

Why had Annie had to move in here? Was it to help take care of her mom? The woman might be a saint. He felt an unfamiliar swell in his chest.

"Well, then," he said, willing the feeling to go away. "I've made up my mind. I can't leave the job unfinished."

Annie studied him, her expression unreadable.

Maybe he'd gone too far. He wasn't sure what had gotten into him. He'd spent the morning anxiously standing outside, sure Bella would need his help. She clearly had done just fine on her own. The twins were healthy and happy, and Bella didn't seem the least bit frazzled.

It wasn't that Bella didn't need him anymore. She just didn't need him in *this* instance. She still needed her dad, even if it was in different ways.

That's what he told himself, at least. And what was this new offer he'd come up with? Was it a need to feel needed? Was he transferring his unwanted help onto Annie and her mom?

Or was it something else? Something to do with the way his heart pounded a little faster when Annie smiled at him. Something with the urge to look away when she flashed those sea-colored eyes at him...

"If you'll have me," he added.

"Of course we'll have you," Clara said. "Maybe you can figure out why our ice maker stopped working, too."

"Mom!" Annie whispered. "You can't just make people fix random things in your house."

"He's not random. He's our neighbor." Clara smiled at him, hands placidly resting on her lap.

"That's right," Miles said with a nod. "Not random at all."

Annie stared at them. "We can't solicit help forever."

"Speak for yourself!" Clara said.

Annie sighed and shook her head. "I'm going to set the table."

Miles smiled to himself. There was nothing better than helping a neighbor.

If it happened to be a pretty neighbor with kind eyes and gentle hands – well, all the better.

Ten

While Annie had warned her mom not to ask about the firefighter dating ads, she had failed to anticipate her mom seeing Miles as a free handyman to use at her will.

The glares Annie shot at her had no effect. She would have a talk with her later. There was absolutely no way she'd allow Miles to fix anything else in their house.

Annie was enough of a charity case. It was embarrassing. She didn't want Miles to know all the broken things they lived with— the doors that didn't close all the way, the ancient appliances that didn't work.

She still had some pride. There was a dash of vanity in her, and she wouldn't let the handsome firefighter from down the street think less of her, if that was even possible.

Annie and Bella wrangled the twins into their highchairs for dinner. Her mom moved steadily to the table and took a seat, but it was obvious she couldn't have lifted Leon or Noel, or done the task of strapping them in. It would be weeks, if not months, before she could safely pick up the twins, or be left alone to watch them.

The realization sat heavily on Annie's chest. It would be hard to keep her mom from getting involved, too, hurting herself further. The whole thing was a mess of her own creation. If only she'd –

"So, Bella," Clara said, sitting back in her seat, "I saw those pictures you put up of your dad. How'd you get his head onto that body?"

Annie nearly dropped a plate of buns.

"*Mom!*" Annie hissed.

Clara put up her hands, palms out, as she shrugged. "What? It looked very real."

"It was real, " Bella said, a devilish smile on her face. "Those are actual pictures of my dad."

"Oh! I thought you had done something on the computer," Clara said. The corners of her mouth curved down and she nodded approvingly. "Very impressive."

Annie didn't know what to do. Her cheeks burned red, her head felt hot, and she couldn't come up with any words to say.

She did the only thing she could think of: she walked back into the kitchen.

Unfortunately, she could still hear what they were talking about.

"Do you often take glamour shots, lying on the fire truck like that?" Clara asked, her voice crackling with laughter.

Annie shut her eyes. If only she could disappear into the kitchen cupboards, or into a dark hole somewhere, and never emerge.

The shame was too heavy, hanging around her neck like an anvil. He was going to know that she'd shown her mom those pictures. He was going to think she was a silly schoolgirl, fawning over him.

Then she heard Miles' laughter.

"No, I do not often lay on the fire truck and take glamour shots."

"You should," Clara said promptly. "You have a knack for it, not to mention the physique."

Annie spun around, daggers coming from her eyes, but no one was looking at her, especially not her mom.

Miles shook his head, rubbing his face in his hand. "It's not a hobby of mine. I did it for the department. We needed to fundraise to repair one of our fire engines. I got talked into doing a firefighter calendar. They promised me no one on the island would ever see the pictures."

Bella snorted a laugh. "And you believed them, Dad? Don't you know pictures on the internet are forever?"

He sighed. "I do now."

Annie walked back into the room, her spine straightened. "Leave him alone, Mom," she said sternly. Then, to Miles, "I'm sorry. You don't have to talk about this."

Miles' eyes met hers. He held her stare for a moment, a smile dancing on his face. "It's okay. It was my own foolishness that got me into this situation, though Bella put a fun twist on it."

He looked at Bella, and she grinned, picking up her sloppy joe and taking a big bite.

"How much did it get you?" asked Clara. "Did you at least get enough money to fix the fire engine?"

He shook his head. "Not even close. The price for replacement parts has skyrocketed."

"Can you get a replacement truck, then?" Annie asked.

"That's even worse. There's a five-year lead time, and the price has gone from $300,000 a few years ago to a cool million dollars today. Ladder trucks are two million now."

Annie gasped. "How can that be?"

"Lots of reasons. There's a private equity company who decided it'd be a good idea to buy up all the suppliers. Once they owned most of it, they increased the prices."

"That's just un-American," Clara said, shaking her head. "Gouging firemen across the country! For heaven's sake."

"Un-American, and possibly monopolistic. We have a case filed by the local prosecuting attorney to sue them for anti-competitive practices."

Annie chanced another look at him. "That's promising."

He nodded. "It is."

"You still don't have a fire engine that works, though," Bella said. "And since I'm so skilled with digital marketing and advertisement, you should let me fundraise for you."

"Not a chance," he said with a grin. "I'm not going to risk seeing my face splashed across the ferries again."

He picked up his sloppy joe, the bun looking comically small in his large hands, and took a bite.

"Annie, this is quite literally the best sloppy joe I've ever had. And these buns."

The redness that had finally receded from her face threatened to return. "Brioche buns. They're key. If you like the recipe, I can send it to you. It's really easy to make."

"Yeah, Dad, get it," Bella said. "This needs to be on our evening rotation."

Miles pulled his phone from his pocket. "Do you mind, Annie?"

Butterflies took off in her stomach. He wanted her number. Just for a recipe, but still. No one had asked for her number in decades. Certainly not a cute firefighter.

It was silly to be excited, but she was going to hang on to this feeling, if only for a little while.

She cleared her throat. "Sure," she said, rattling off her number.

They finished dinner without further incident, and Bella and Miles stayed afterwards to help clean up, despite Annie's protests.

They didn't have a dishwasher, but Miles had worked in a restaurant in his younger years and was surprisingly efficient. Bella was like a trained busser, clearing the table, drying the dishes, and then putting them away.

"We need to hire you two on full time," Clara said.

Annie let the comment go. Her nagging had no effect, the twins needed their baths, and her mom needed to relax whether she wanted to admit it or not.

Annie refused Bella's offer to help with the kids, thanked her again, and slipped her some cash for her time.

"Thank you so much," she beamed. "I'll put this right into the Babysitters Club fund."

Miles eyed her warily. "How much are you charging? I think we need to talk fair rates."

Annie smiled. "It was more than fair. She's a huge help."

Bella beamed. "I'd probably do it for free, but that wouldn't be very good business practice for the Babysitters Club."

Annie nodded solemnly. "It wouldn't be."

Bella disappeared through the door, and Miles lingered for a moment, his tall figure looming against the dark evening sky.

"Thanks for taking her on," he said.

"It's my pleasure. Honestly, I love having her around."

He paused, his gaze so intent that it set the butterflies off again.

"We both love being around," he said, his voice low and husky.

Annie gaped at him, blinking. He was so close, leaning in, it seemed like he was going to hug her goodbye.

Or kiss her.

No, that was absurd.

Still, the thought of it rendered her speechless. "Oh," she finally managed to choke out.

He flashed a smile and nodded a goodbye before ducking out of the doorway.

•   •   •

That night, as she lay in bed next to her snoring mother, Annie saw that smile every time she closed her eyes. He was the hunky firefighter calendar come to life, his sultry gaze, his deep, quiet voice.

We both love being around.

What did he mean by that? Was it the sloppy joes? It couldn't be. They weren't that good.

It had to be about Bella. Miles lit up when she was nearby, or when he talked about her. Even when Bella made snippy comments at him, he didn't flinch. He was her biggest fan. He was proud of her new babysitting endeavor, as he should be. She was an incredibly fast learner, and she kept a great attitude.

Annie wasn't going to let herself think it had anything to do with *her*. To Bella's dismay, Miles wasn't interested in dating, and he surely wasn't interested in Annie.

It was time to embrace her new reality. Annie was at her absolute lowest point. She thought making the decision to end things with Roy would be bottom, or the long divorce process, but no. Those were just the steps to where she was now – a dark, cold, rock bottom.

Living with her mother, barely able to pay her bills, scouring for hand-me-down clothes for the kids, all while Roy lived his life essentially unchanged.

The thought of him flared her temper, heat flickering in her chest – but she wasn't going to focus on that. Bitterness didn't get her anywhere. It only grew more bitterness, and she didn't need any more negativity.

It was silly for her to entertain the idea that Miles might be interested in her. Not only because he was a muscular, square-jawed Greek god of a hero firefighter, but because she was not in the place to entertain a romance. She probably never would be, just like her jeans would never fit again. She'd perpetually have yogurt in her hair, and she'd always live in this little house with her mom.

Still. That night, she could think only of him, and as she sat at work the next day, the absurdity of their fire department being out a firetruck was stuck in her mind.

She got an idea, and there was only one person to call with an idea.

"Good morning!" Margie's voice chirped over the phone, "How are you, Annie?"

"I'm good. How are you?"

"Very good."

Annie cleared her throat. "Listen, I wanted to talk to you about something. I heard about the fire department needing to raise money to fix the fire engine."

"Yes, Hank talks about it all the time. It's a real problem for the community."

Annie took a deep breath. "What if we held a fundraiser? A gala at Saltwater Cove? We could do it before your busy season starts up again, and…"

Margie squealed, "That's a wonderful idea. I don't know why I hadn't thought of it. I've been so busy with weddings, but yes, absolutely!"

"I want to help plan it," Annie said firmly.

Margie was quiet for a moment. "Sure, but honey, you have a lot on your plate."

"I do, but..." Annie had to take the blob of thoughts she'd been chewing over and force them into words. It was no easy task for an overtired mind, one she was sure would never sleep through the night again. "I don't want to be excluded from life. I feel isolated enough as it is. I need to give back somehow."

That was the most she could croak out. She didn't know if it made sense, or if it justified the depth of her feelings, but there it was. Out in the open.

"Of course, I won't exclude you!" Margie said. "I understand. Believe me, I understand."

Warmth flooded her chest. "You do?"

"Better than you know." Margie cleared her throat. "Okay, I have some contacts and I can start getting some things together. Maybe we can meet up this week to discuss it? Bella can watch the kids, maybe with your mom?"

Bella can watch the kids. It was that easy. She lived just down the street, so she could pop in to help.

Annie felt the skies above her clearing. She would be able to leave the house without worrying about the kids and her mom becoming grievously injured. She could have time to something – anything. Maybe even a haircut!

A weight lifted off Annie's chest. "I would love that."

"Lovely! I'll be in touch!"

Annie ended the call, her chest buoyant and light.

Eleven

After he left Annie's house that night, his words echoed for days.

We both love being around.

Miles didn't know what had prompted him to say it. It felt like a confession, one he wasn't prepared to admit even to himself.

It had snuck up on him. Never in the fourteen years since Madeline's passing had he felt the sort of stir in his chest that he felt now.

When Annie smiled at him, or laughed at one of his jokes, or by God, just looked at him, the emotions rose so quickly they threatened to spin into a tornado.

He'd never lived in tornado country. He didn't have a safe room. He'd never even seen the movie *Twister.* He was completely unprepared for handling a tornado, and thus walked right into it like an oaf.

It was true that he loved fixing things. He'd done so much to his own house that he was running out of projects. Plus, when he was at Annie's place, he got to see Bella in action. Why not fix a few windows to get more of that?

If he was being forced to reflect on his out-of-the-blue declaration, that wasn't what made him *love* being around.

The truth was, it was simply nice at Annie's house. Even though the house was small and overflowing with toys, it was warm. Full of life. Full of love. He and Bella had a happy home, but it wasn't as exciting as Annie's. He missed the energy young kids brought – chaos, yes, but so much fun.

There was mystery, too. Every time he saw Annie's mouth curving in a half smile, he had to know what she was thinking. He needed to know her story. Why had she taken her mom in – or why had her mom taken her in? How did she end up a single mother? What were her hopes, her dreams?

For some inexplicable reason, his mind kept inventing an image of the two of them staying up late at night, confessing even more to each other.

Bella still had emails flooding in with women telling their life stories – framing themselves as victims or heroes – but the only one Miles wanted to know about was Annie.

The day after having dinner together, he texted her and thanked her for the recipe.

Getting her number was a brilliant move. He couldn't stop patting himself on the back for it. Yeah, he'd make the recipe, but now he could talk to her at any time.

She didn't write back until after eight. He told himself she didn't have time before that; it was when the twins went to sleep.

"I'm so glad you liked it," she wrote. "I'm happy to share other recipes I've accumulated over the years, especially the kid-friendly ones. Though I'm sure Bella has a more complex palate than Leon and Noel."

"You might be surprised."

He paused. How to do this without being awkward? He wanted to spend more time with her. He had to know more about her. But he couldn't very well invite himself over unless...

"I wanted to ask – when is a good time for me to come back and fix up those things your mom mentioned?"

He hit send, and within seconds, she was typing a response, the three dots bouncing on his screen.

But then, she stopped.

Typed again.

Stopped.

She was thinking. Perhaps about his entire obvious scheme. Perhaps debating how to politely tell him to buzz off.

His heart rate picked up.

When her response came in, he jumped to read it. "That's kind of you, but don't feel obligated to fix anything. My mom is just... a mom."

He grinned, the glow of the phone illuminating his face. "I know. I get it, but I'd really like to help. You've been great with Bella, and she's been so happy. I insist." He paused. Might as well go for it. "I have Monday off. How is nine?"

The dots appeared again. Miles held his breath.

"Well...if you really insist, I have a research day and I'll be working from home. It might be easier with the twins at daycare."

"Yes!" he whispered, then wrote back. "Great! See you then."

He didn't tell Bella what he'd be up to. She was going to be at school, and he didn't need to explain himself. Most of all, he didn't need her to ask questions.

He arrived on Annie's doorstep with an enormous bag of tools and knocked.

"Maintenance is back," he said when Annie opened the door.

"Finally. I've been waiting all day!"

She was dressed in a soft-looking white sweater and a pair of loose, light-colored jeans. Her hair was in a ponytail, wisps being blown loose by the wind.

He grinned at her, and there it was – that smile.

His chest constricted. Miles lowered his eyes as he walked in.

"Can I offer you something to drink? Tea or coffee?"

He set his tool bag down. "Tea would be great."

She nodded, disappearing into the kitchen. "You'll be happy to know my mom isn't here to torment you again. She volunteers at the library on Mondays." Annie re-entered the room. "I wanted to apologize about her asking about...well, you know, the *thing*."

His eyebrows shot up. "What thing?"

She let out a sigh. "You know... the dating ad."

"Oh!" A laugh burst out of him. "That was nothing. I'm getting it much worse at work. Every time I open a drawer, or look in the fridge, a copy of Bella's fine work stares back at me."

Annie scrunched her nose. "That's rough."

"It is. My own fault, though. I can't even blame Bella."

Annie looked at him, her expression placid, and the tornado winds picked up. He couldn't stop himself from talking. Rambling really.

"Two years ago, Bella got on this kick. She wanted me to start dating, and now she's escalated. She says I have to get married and get her a new mom."

Annie's eyes widened. "That's a big ask."

"It is. I told her she has a mom."

"Is she still involved in your lives?"

Miles shook his head. "She passed away shortly after Bella was born."

Annie's expression fell. "I'm so sorry. I had no idea."

"It's okay. It was a long time ago," he lied.

He always said that. He didn't want to make people feel bad, but to him, it had just happened. In his dreams, he saw the blinding lights of the OR, the chill in the air, the bleeding they couldn't stop.

"I'm sure this is just some sort of passing teenage whim," he added. "I made it clear that I won't be remarrying or dating until she's out of the house – or never, to be honest."

There. That should do it. Even if he couldn't convince himself that these feelings were meaningless, he could at least try to convince Annie that his intentions here were purely janitorial.

Annie laughed. "I hear you on that. I've just gone through a divorce myself, and I can't imagine doing any of it again." She stopped. "I mean, of course, what you went through is much worse. I'm not trying to compare – "

He held up a hand. "I didn't take it that way."

The tea kettle went off, and she disappeared again, leaving Miles to grapple with the sinking feeling in his chest.

The winds had died down. A divorce. She'd never do it again.

Talk about a clear message.

Then again, if he didn't want to date or marry again, why was he so disappointed she didn't want to, either?

Twelve

"Does your ex-husband live nearby?"

"He's in Seattle." Annie handed him a mug of tea. "Would you like some lemon or milk?"

He shook his head and murmured a thanks. "That's a long trip for a pair of two-year-olds."

He flashed her a smile, his brows low over his eyes.

The tension in her chest eased as Annie took a seat. Miles got it. How could Roy not?

"It's tough," she admitted.

Annie wasn't going to pull him into her drama. She was not going to be the bitter ex-wife, dumping her problems on people who were only asking polite questions.

His eye lingered on hers. "How often does he make the trip?"

His smoldering gaze threatened to pull her in, though.

She stared back at him, trying to decide how much to say. "About once a month."

One side of his mouth tipped up. "A dedicated father."

She broke first, a small laugh escaping her. "I take the twins over early on a Saturday, and he brings them back on a Sunday. It's not been easy on them."

"One night a month? It must not be easy on him either."

Oh. Of course Miles would sympathize with Roy. He was a father, too. He'd see his side of things; he'd think about how much Roy must miss the kids.

Annie sucked in a breath to explain herself, but Miles went on before she could form a word.

"The poor guy must lose so much sleep – the one night a month they're with him."

Annie laughed again. "You almost had me there."

Miles took a sip of tea, a smile dancing on his lips. "Sorry, I – I hear about these kinds of dads and it blows my mind. I would die if I had to be away from Bella even half the time."

"Thank goodness you'll never let her go to college," Annie said.

His smile was unchanged. "Exactly. She's not the type. I've always discouraged her from growing up or following her dreams, especially if it takes her away from me."

"That's healthy."

"Isn't it?" He grinned.

This wouldn't do. If she stayed any longer, that gorgeous smile beaming at her, those broad shoulders shaking as he laughed, she'd melt into a puddle.

Or worse, she'd confide in him even more.

"Would you want some cookies with your tea?"

"Sure."

In the kitchen, her face nearly touching the cabinet, Annie forced herself to take a deep breath. *Do not make a fool of your-*

self, she silently whispered as she grabbed two packs of Lorna Doones.

"Are these okay?"

His eyes widened. "I love a Lorna. Or a pack of Lornas—let's be honest."

Impressively muscular and in shape, but not so much that he'd refuse a pack of cookies. Annie realized then and there that was her new type. Not whatever zero body fat thing Roy had gotten into.

She handed him a pack and opened one for herself.

"One night a month." He unwrapped the cookies carefully, resting them in his big hands. "Is that all he wanted?"

"We never put together a formal custody agreement." Annie paused. "After he insisted on moving to Seattle – "

He cut her off. "He insisted on moving to Seattle? Why?"

She really shouldn't tell him all of this. But how often did she come across a sympathetic ear? How often were people not uncomfortable when they heard about the divorce? Especially people on the island who had known Roy growing up. They'd make excuses, or make an awkward face and try to rush away.

"It was a big factor in our divorce, actually. We both grew up on the island. We were high school sweethearts, and we moved back to be closer to my mom. To have help. He said it was the most beautiful place on earth and he'd missed it."

"At least he was right about that," Miles said with a nod.

Annie went on. "After the twins were born, he got overwhelmed with it all. He told me he needed to keep an apartment in Seattle so he could have time away from the family to improve himself, and that he'd use our house as his home base."

Shock registered on Miles' face, his eyebrows shooting up and his mouth opening slightly. "Well, if that isn't a load of – " Miles stopped himself, clearing his throat. "Sorry. I have no sympathy for deadbeat dads."

Annie couldn't get the smile off her face. She dipped a cookie in her tea and took a bite. It melted in her mouth.

He stared at her. "I'm sorry, is that too far?"

She looked up, unable to stop the smile crossing her lips. "No, it's just...I feel bad. Like I'm gossiping about him."

"Is it gossip? Or are those the facts?"

The facts. That was it. As much as she turned it over in her head, as many times as she'd doubted herself, these were the things Roy had said, those were the actions Roy had taken. She'd presented it exactly as it had happened.

Annie set down her tea. "I get that having twins is intense. Believe me, I've been here for it all. But he gave up so quickly, and I didn't – I never thought he'd crumble like that. I'd known him for most of my life, and nothing about him screamed 'I'm going to run away at the first sign of trouble.'"

And worst of all, people still blamed *her*. Like she should've known he would act like that, like she should've chosen a better man.

She wasn't going to mention any of that.

"It's not you," he said, as if reading her mind. "It's a tale as old as time. Dad going out for milk and all. Don't blame yourself. Some people can take the heat, and some people can't."

A mischievous smile lit his face.

"You'd know all about that, wouldn't you?" she asked.

"I know a thing or two about heat," he said, lifting his shoulder with the slightest hint of a shrug.

Was he flirting? Or was she losing her mind?

The tea was overheating her. Or he was overheating her.

Annie took a gulp of tea, letting the burn bring her back to earth. "How long have you been a firefighter? And would you say it's a calling?"

He smiled, the warmth reaching his eyes for a brief moment. "Six years. I got interested in it when I became a dad. I felt powerless to prevent bad things from happening to the people I loved." He scrubbed his jaw with his hand, pausing, as though weighing his words. "Madeline died in a freak accident. An amniotic embolism minutes after Bella was born. There was really nothing that could have been done, but part of me felt like if I'd been more prepared, I could have saved her."

"I'm so sorry." Annie could feel tears pricking at the backs of her eyes. She remembered only too well how vulnerable pregnancy and childbirth was, how aware she was that at any moment, it could all go terribly wrong.

"From that day forward, I felt like I had to protect Bella from everything. And, for some reason, I kept having nightmares about fires." He laughed. "So, I guess in a way, it's a calling. I started as a volunteer, became an EMT, and eventually got hired on full time."

"That's incredible. Really."

He shrugged, eyes averted to his remaining cookies.

She sat back. "Well, I had an idea, and I was hoping I could tell you in person."

"Oh?" He raised an eyebrow, his eyes smoldering with playfulness.

That scowl. He was ridiculously handsome. It shouldn't be allowed.

"I think it's absurd you don't have a working firetruck. I talked to Margie, and we're going to hold a fundraiser – a gala at Saltwater Cove."

His expression brightened. "Really?"

She nodded, her voice picking up speed. "I don't know how much we can raise, so I'm sure it won't solve all of your problems, but Margie is pretty good at these things, and I'm going to help."

"That's incredibly kind of you. All of us at the station will appreciate it." He stood abruptly. "All right, enough gossiping between us girls."

She laughed.

He went on, "I'm going to get to work on that window, then I'm going to hit everything else that your mom listed off for me."

Annie shook her head. "It'll take weeks."

"I've got weeks," he said.

Her heart leapt at the idea. Weeks of having Miles at her house, sauntering around in those t-shirts, biceps lifting those tools up and down, up and down.

It was like a dream come true. Annie couldn't believe it was real.

. . .

Except it was real. Over the next three weeks, Miles was at her house every chance he had. Whenever he had a day off, he showed up with his tool bag, more supplies, and more sassy comments about Roy.

After the second week, Annie started to question whether the fire department really had so many extra home improvement parts lying around.

All he'd say on the matter was, "I cannot reveal my sources."

If she could've afforded to pay him back, she would have – not that he would have accepted it.

Annie rearranged her work from home days so she could be there with him as much as possible. They passed the time gossiping, laughing, and trying to keep Annie's mom from adding more items to the list.

She'd meant to host him for dinner again, but things got so hectic with work and planning the gala that the idea got away from her.

Then he beat her to it. "I've got the holiday off, and I want to invite you, the kids, and your mom over for a Thanksgiving feast."

It was too much. Too kind, and altogether too... enticing.

"I wouldn't want to impose," Annie said.

He shook his head. "My parents never come for Thanksgiving, and Madeline's parents are long gone. It's usually just me and Bella, unless we invite some of her friends."

Annie cocked her head. He seemed like someone who would have a big, happy, warm family all around him. "Really?"

"Really. You'd be doing us a favor."

Annie scoffed. "If you want chocolate melted into your carpets, sure."

"As a matter of fact, I do," he said, staring her down.

Annie let out a little laugh. He was serious! Who was she to deny him?

"What can I bring?" she asked.

He held up a hand. "Absolutely nothing. You are my guest. Bring your mother, bring your kids, bring an appetite."

She grinned at him. He was impossible to argue with. "Okay, if you insist."

Thirteen

As it was, Miles had already said too much about Roy. He had to stop himself from going on rants.

Yet how could he stay quiet? The guy was a despicable coward.

Having twins wasn't easy, but how did Roy think Annie felt? How could this guy decide it was all too much for him, then run off to the city and leave his wife and kids?

And to tell Annie he'd use the island as his home base because he needed his own space? The audacity was unreal.

Heat crept up Miles' neck every time he thought about it.

Maybe that was why he couldn't stop talking about it. He found Roy's behavior so ridiculous, so outrageous that he was compelled to tell Annie. She needed to know it wasn't her fault. She needed to know any reasonable person who heard her side of the story would feel the same outrage.

What was Roy's side of the story? What story did he tell himself? That Annie refused to move to Seattle, and that was why he didn't see his kids?

He could tell Annie tried to hold herself back. She stayed polite. She didn't want to "gossip." As far as Miles was concerned, Annie wasn't outraged enough.

Whatever the reason, it didn't matter. He had to let it go and focus his attention on Thanksgiving, and on not bringing it up again. Bella was thrilled when she heard they'd be hosting Annie's little family.

"Do you think the twins would like pumpkin pie?" she asked.

"I think they would love pumpkin pie," Miles told her.

She grinned. "I'm gonna make everything from scratch, even the crust," she said. "I'll need your credit card to get this place ready. It's not fit for guests."

Normally he wouldn't hand his card over for such a request, but she was right. They hadn't hosted in years. Last year, they'd taken an Alaskan cruise during Bella's holiday break. It had been an epic adventure, but it left them without proper placemats, as Bella pointed out.

When Thanksgiving arrived, Miles could admit they'd both gone a bit overboard. Bella went all out on the house: rich wine-colored linens for the table, monogrammed cloth napkins, golden turkey napkin rings, new dishes and serving platters, and an ornate turkey-shaped candelabra where the long candles made up the turkey's tail feathers. She also bought an apron for Miles, head chef, with a turkey face prominently displayed on his chest.

For his part, Miles cooked two turkeys – one in the oven, and one deep fried. He made vegetarian and non-vegetarian stuffing, mashed potatoes and candied sweet potatoes, roasted Brussels sprouts with a balsamic drizzle, homemade dinner rolls, corn bread, and just for kicks, a side of sloppy joes.

That was for the twins. He wasn't sure what they'd like from the spread, so he'd made something he knew they'd enjoy.

To top it off, he crafted a fall-inspired sangria and covered half of the kitchen island with an extensive charcuterie spread with various cheeses, meats, nuts, and dried fruit. The twins had their own charcuterie board with crackers, mozzarella cheese, and bites of chocolate.

It was enough food to feed the fire station, but he couldn't help himself. Before dinner, he sent Bella down to help Annie pack up the twins, their highchairs, and her mom.

Miles stayed back, putting on the finishing touches as he transferred the sides to their fancy new dishes, soft music playing in the background.

The door opened and a flurry of noise poured into the peaceful kitchen.

"Okay, okay," Clara repeated loudly. "Noel, I will pick you up after Leon's turn is done."

"NO!" she screamed.

"Mom, you're not supposed to be picking them up anyway. They're too heavy," Annie said.

"Nonsense. I feel great."

Miles filled two glasses with sangria, making sure to throw in a few cranberries, and walked out to greet them.

"Happy Thanksgiving!" he called.

Annie looked up, catching his eye as she took off her coat. She wore a velvet red dress, the fabric catching the light with her every move, clinging to her curves like liquid silk.

Miles' breath caught in his chest.

Luckily, Bella was able to speak. "Hey, everyone! Let me take your coats. Leon, Noel, I have a surprise for you."

She took Noel by the hand and led her to a large, wooden chest labeled TOYS. Clara followed, carrying Leon.

If Miles had his wits about him, he would've realized the chest was new, and that Bella had filled it with toys.

Instead, his eyes were on Annie. He handed her a glass of sangria, his hand brushing hers, his skin burning at her touch. She whispered a thank you before turning her attention to the toy scene unfolding before them.

Clara took her glass of sangria out of his hand without a word.

Bella popped the chest open, pulled out a set of large Lego blocks, and dumped them all over the floor. "Ta-da!"

Noel immediately forgot her claim on Clara and dropped to the floor. Leon watched suspiciously from his grand-mother's arms.

"Whenever you're ready, Leon, we can build a tower together," Bella said in a sing-song voice.

He hid his grinning face in Clara's hair.

Annie stepped closer, her gray eyes twinkling with a smile. "It didn't feel right coming empty-handed, so I got this bottle of wine and a bottle of sparkling cider for Bella."

Miles accepted them, willing himself to find words. "Thank you. You're – that's lovely."

Uh oh. That was a close one. He'd almost bumbled like the fool he was.

"It smells amazing in here," she added.

He forced himself to not stare. "I hope you came hungry. I've got a charcuterie board on the kitchen island for the grown-ups and," he turned and grabbed the small plastic tray, "a small charcuterie board for little hands."

Annie's mouth dropped open. "That's adorable! Kids, look!"

They did not look, but her eyes drifted up to him.

Warmth spread through his chest. He wanted to show her the rest, the urge tugging at him like an overeager terrier.

"I don't want them to make a mess in your living room," she said, frowning.

He waved a hand and put the tray on the ottoman. "I'm not worried about it."

Leon, now on his own two feet, walked over to investigate and selected a piece of mozzarella cheese before taking a bite.

Bella tried to entice Noel to have some chocolate, but she was completely focused on building a Lego tower.

Miles nodded toward the kitchen. "Shall we?"

They followed him, and both Annie and Clara exclaimed when they saw the charcuterie board.

"Is this dinner?" Clara asked, a grin on her face.

"Of course not," he said, handing them each a plate. "We've got two turkeys to eat."

"Two?" Annie stared at him. "You're joking."

"They're small," he clarified. "The big ones dry out too much."

"Come on Annie, relax!" Clara said, taking a seat at the kitchen island. She jerked her thumb in Annie's direction. "This girl never relaxes."

"I relax," Annie said, still standing.

Clara went on. "What better time than when someone else is cooking for you?"

"You cook for me all the time." Annie leaned on the doorway, glancing at the twins.

"Of course I do! I'm your mother. But you know this is special. It's not every day that a – "

Annie cut her off. "Can I help with anything, Miles?"

A smile tugged at the corner of his mouth. What was Clara going to say? That a what? Neighbor? Firefighter? Decent guy cooked for her?

He had a tendency to go overboard with these sorts of things, but this time maybe he'd gone extra overboard. Maybe there was a part of him that was trying to show up her ex-husband. Maybe he wanted Annie to know the sort of treatment she deserved.

Maybe he needed to keep that to himself. "The turkeys are resting, so we can sit down to dinner in about twenty minutes. Or later. Whatever you want! You're our honored guests!"

The evening evolved into a wonderful chaos, first with fitting all the food onto the table, then getting everyone into their seats. The twins sat in their highchairs for a full sixteen minutes, eating bits of cheese and globs of sloppy joe before working their way back into the living room.

With Bella by his side, Leon wasn't frightened at all. She became a magician, pulling out new toys every time one of the twins threatened to lose interest.

"When did you get all of these?" Miles asked.

She shrugged. "When you gave me your credit card, I reasoned it should be an investment into my business."

He nodded. "I see that."

"An unwilling investor," Clara said, snorting a laugh.

Miles grinned. There was nothing unwilling about it. Unknowing, maybe, but not unwilling.

After dinner, there was far too much food left over.

Miles had planned for it. He'd bought containers to make meals for Annie and Clara to freeze.

"If you don't have room in your freezer, I've got a chest freezer in the garage." He paused, carving knife mid-air. "Unless you didn't like the food. Then I won't force it on you."

"We like the food," Clara said, pointing a finger at him. "Pack it up!"

"Mom!" Annie hissed, but even she couldn't help but smile. "Thank you," she said. "That's very thoughtful."

Focused on his work, he almost missed Clara's announcement ten minutes later. "The twins are getting tired. I'm going to take them home and put them to bed."

Annie, who had insisted on helping clear the table, set down a pile of dishes. "Let me finish up in here and we can go."

"Nonsense!" Clara said. "Bella, you'll help me, won't you?"

Her answer was instantaneous. "I'd love to!"

"But – "

"And you, young lady," Clara said, scowling at Annie. "Try to imagine how differently this night would go if you were all the way over in Seattle."

Annie couldn't get a word in before her mother disappeared.

Miles pretended to focus on packing the rest of the leftovers as the twins were dressed and ushered outside.

When the door shut, it was quiet enough to hear the music again.

"Well, I am going to stay to help you clean up," Annie announced.

He sighed. "Always the cleaning with you."

She caught his eye and he winked as a laugh burst from her. He felt his chest swell. He needed more of that laugh.

Fourteen

Could her mom be any more obvious? Annie glaring at her had zero effect. Clara was convinced Miles was interested in her, and she'd contrived this situation to prove it.

It was nonsense. Annie knew that. Miles had made it clear to her in a polite, but pointed, way when he told her he had no interest in dating. His focus was clearly on his daughter, as it should be.

"Then why is he making excuses to fix things for us?" Clara had argued.

"Probably because you demanded it," Annie told her. "And he feels bad we live in a shoe."

This was the truth, and Annie knew it. Miles was a charismatic, hunky, brave firefighter who had half of Skagit and the entirety of San Juan county chasing after him. He wanted no part of being set up with anyone, especially not a sad sack mom like her.

Still. It was impossible not to stare at him, especially in the warm glow of the kitchen lights, his soulful brown eyes glancing up at her every now and again.

If only the women who pined after his dating ad could see him in person. He was even more mesmerizing in real life. They wouldn't be able to bear it – Annie hardly could. That ridiculous apron accentuated how large he was, barely covering his chest, his biceps bulging under his maroon sweater.

Miles pulled out the bottle of wine she'd brought and lifted it to eye level. "Eh?"

She really shouldn't. It had been ages since she'd had a sip of anything and she had no tolerance for alcohol. She'd already had a glass of sangria, and that had gone right to her head.

Then again, she'd eaten her weight in potatoes. That had to count for something. "Sure, why not? I've apparently got a babysitter tonight."

He clapped his hands. "That's the Thanksgiving spirit!"

She flashed a smile at him and took a seat at the island. He pulled out a tall wine glass and set it in front of her with a clink on the granite. The glass was quickly filled with ruby red liquid.

What was one glass of wine? The sooner she went home, the sooner she'd have to hear her mom go on about the elaborate, thoughtful meal he'd made for them.

Not only had he cooked enough food to feed an army, he'd made special foods just for the twins. And that little charcuterie board! It was the sweetest thing she'd ever seen.

Enough to make a woman swoon.

"What's this about you moving to Seattle?" he asked, sliding the wine glass toward her.

Annie picked it up, the weight of it substantial in her hand. "Just the same pressure from Roy. He's convinced all our problems would be solved if I would agree to move to the city."

"*Our* problems," Miles repeated.

A smile tugged at the corner of her lips. She took a sip of wine, her mouth flooded with plum and oak.

This was an old favorite of hers. Inexpensive, but rich. Annie couldn't remember the last time she'd had a glass.

Miles cleared his throat. "I'm sorry if it seems like I'm overly harsh on him. I've seen his tricks before."

"Roy's tricks in particular?" she asked, raising an eyebrow.

"Well, not him, exactly," he said. "But the playbook. My dad did the same thing. Came up with some excuses and and left one day."

Annie's heart sank. No wonder he was being so nice to her. He felt bad for her because she reminded him of *his mom*.

Humbling for Annie, to be sure. Worse for him.

She set her wine glass down. "I'm so sorry, Miles."

He waved a hand, scrunching up the left side of his handsome face. "It only made me stronger. My mom raised me on her own. We didn't need him."

"I hope my kids feel the same way," she said quietly. "Because it doesn't seem like he's in any rush to get to know them."

His eyes latched onto hers. "It's his mistake. And yes, they will feel the same way."

"I shouldn't say anything." She sighed. "If I moved, I'm sure he'd see them more often. They love seeing him. They *need* to see him."

"Funny how the onus is on you to make it easier for him, though."

Annie flinched, crossing her arms over her chest. Any time she spoke badly of Roy, a sinking guilt hit her immediately. Roy could still make her question herself. Was it her fault he didn't see the twins more? Or was it his?

Did it have to be anyone's fault? She needed to be mature and do what was best for the twins. If that was moving to Seattle, then so be it.

"I think," he said gently, "your mom is onto something. Moving there, being removed from everyone who knows and loves you – that's not nothing."

She bit her lip. He had a point—it was one of the thoughts she wrestled with constantly. It wasn't just finding a place to live that she could afford, or finding a new job. She'd have to find a new support system, if that was even possible.

"I know."

Landslide by Fleetwood Mac carried over the speakers and Annie gasped, putting a hand to her chest. "I *love* this song."

"Me too." He stepped forward, his hand outstretched, "Shall we?"

Her heart took off in her chest. "Here?"

"Why not?" He untied his apron and tossed it onto the kitchen counter.

She stood from the kitchen stool, her head spinning. Was it the wine, or was she swooning?

It was unlike her to swoon. It couldn't be that.

There wasn't time to dwell on it. She put her hand into his, the skin of his palms rough and warm, and he led her to an open spot near the dining room table.

Annie placed a hand on the back of his neck. He put his hand around her waist and gently pulled her closer, his massive frame swaying left, then right, guiding her.

How could someone so large be so graceful?

"I'm not trying to influence you," he said, his voice low.

His face was so near hers, but she'd have to stand on her tiptoes to close the distance. The thought made the breath catch in her throat.

"I know," she said. "I want to do the right thing. I just don't know what that is."

He stared at her intently, his face unreadable.

She was spurred to speak again. "Thank you so much for having us. Everything was delicious, and Bella was so welcoming. I felt like royalty."

A smile hitched the corner of his mouth. He leaned his head closer to hers and dropped his voice. "I'm glad to hear it. It's no less than you deserve."

Her heart pounded in her chest. What did he mean by it all? Was this more of him feeling bad for her?

Annie's head spun, and she stared up at him, unable to break away from his eyes.

The front door opened with a creak.

"I'm back!" Bella's voice called out.

They flew apart, with Annie standing like a fool and Miles almost teleporting next to the kitchen sink.

"That was fast," Miles said.

Bella walked in, her hair tousled. "Those little ones were so tired. We got them in bed as fast as we could, and they were asleep within minutes."

Nothing seemed to register on Bella's face. No recognition of seeing them dance, no hint of the weirdness in the air. Thank goodness.

Annie forced a smile. "That's amazing. Thank you so much, Bella."

"No problem. It was my pleasure." She turned to face her father. "Now, Dad, you promised me we could look at that dating application that came in last week."

Annie's heart sunk. On the positive side, Bella hadn't noticed the energy between them. Unfortunately, it meant her nation-wide search for her new mom was still on.

He scratched an eyebrow with his thumb. "I don't think that's what I said."

"Yes it is! I mean, close enough." She rolled her eyes. "I don't care. I'm getting my laptop."

She took off up the stairs.

Silence hung between them like a dark cloak. Annie took a breath and looked at him. He was staring at her with an intense expression.

"I should get going." Annie walked to the closet.

He was instantly at her side. "I'm sorry," he said, voice low, "I didn't mean to – "

She shook her head. "No, please. It was – "

She paused. What was she trying to say? She didn't know what he was apologizing for. The magical night? The delicious food and wine? Swaying her so gently in his big arms?

"I think," he said slowly, "I got carried away. I'm sorry."

Of course. Apologizing for everything. Getting too close. Being too handsome.

He had to know the effect he had.

"Yeah, me too," Annie said in a hushed voice.

"I wouldn't want Bella getting the wrong idea," he continued. "You know. I've made it pretty clear that I'm not going to entertain her ideas of dating."

Oh, what a fool she was.

It was like a bucket of ice cold water had been splashed onto her head. Any dizzy feeling from the wine evaporated, replaced with being smacked back down to earth.

How could she – even for a moment, there in his arms – how could she have thought he might feel something for her? That he might want to disrupt this life of his, these plans, for her?

Annie made sure the smile was frozen on her face. "Of course."

Bella reentered the room. "She's a firefighter, dad! What more could you ask for?"

"Bella – " he said, his tone serious.

"I have to get going. Thank you both," Annie said, pulling on her coat. "It was a magical night."

What possessed her to say that, she didn't know. But there it was, left hanging in their foyer.

Annie spun, pulling open the door and plunging into the cold evening air.

. . .

The next day, Annie couldn't stop replaying the night in her head, over and over. She managed to avoid questioning from her mom, somehow, with a cursory, "I helped him clean up and that was the end of it."

She didn't ask any questions. It was miraculous, really.

They were getting lunch together for the twins when a honk rang out outside.

Annie peeked through the window and saw Lauren waving excitedly from the driver's seat of a red Porsche.

"What is this!" Annie said, opening the front door.

"I got a new car, baby!" Lauren yelled. "I just got off the ferry. I thought I'd see if I could take you to lunch to thank you for all those rides."

She gaped at her. "Right now?"

Annie's mom appeared behind her. "Oh, go on. I'll do lunch and naps. I'm good for it, I swear."

"I don't know – "

Her mom disappeared, returning a moment later with her coat.

"I need to say bye to the kids," Annie said. She popped her head into the house. "Leon, Noel! I'll be back in just a little bit."

They glanced up at her, then returned to their game of jumping on the couch pillows on the floor.

She went to the car and took a seat. "Lauren, this is so fancy!"

"I know! I'm honestly just looking for excuses to drive around," she said with a laugh.

Annie nodded, her eyes drifting down the street toward Miles' house. She hadn't heard from him since she'd left so abruptly. He probably thought she was rude. Or he was busy picking out his future wife from the pile of Miss America contestants Bella had found for him.

"Uh, hello, are you okay?" Lauren asked.

Annie's head snapped over, looking at her. "Sorry."

"Long night?"

She shifted on the smooth leather seat. "Not exactly."

"What's going on? Is everything okay with Roy?"

Roy. She'd completely forgotten about him for once.

"It's not him. I think...I have a crush on someone."

"Shut up! Good for you. Who is it?"

Annie shook her head, smiling. There was no one else to talk about this to. Her head was overflowing with the events of the night. "Oh you know, the same guy every woman on the island has a crush on."

Lauren gasped. "That firefighter dating guy, Mike?"

"Miles," Annie corrected. "And yes."

Lauren paused. "Did he mention anything about the lawsuit?"

"No, why?"

Lauren cleared her throat. "No reason."

"I know the case was thrown out," Annie said. "My mom told me."

"Yup. Dismissed. There's nothing else they can do," Lauren said.

"You sound like you're happy about it. Like you're against the firefighter," Annie said with a laugh.

She shrugged. "Listen Annie, it's all well and good to help the local fire department or whatever, but why do you assume that the firefighters are right about this? Who are they to get in the way of a good business plan?"

Annie turned to her, blinking. Was Lauren serious? She couldn't be serious. "Because it's not a good business plan. It's a monopoly. A pretty obvious one."

Lauren kept her eyes forward. "That's not what the judge thought."

"Do you know that judge? You can't be on the side of the private equity company."

"I'm on the side of the law. And yes, Judge Henly and I work together. He made the right choice in throwing the case out."

Annie was too stunned to counter, and Lauren quickly changed the subject. They had lunch in town, with Lauren insisting on paying before dropping Annie back off at home.

When she walked in the door, her mom was in one piece, and the twins were asleep.

"Now where did she get the money for that car?" her mom asked, staring out the window, her hands wrapped around a mug of tea.

"I have no idea," Annie said.

Something told her she didn't want to know.

Fifteen

After the Thanksgiving festivities, Margie's family cleared out and went their separate ways, leaving the house feeling infinitely too large and entirely too empty.

Thankfully, she had the firefighter fundraiser to focus on, and she threw herself into it. Sheila had asked to join the planning, and that Sunday, they met at the tea shop.

It was a blustery, quiet day, and their table was tucked away in the English-themed tearoom. Patty served a three-tiered stand containing apple oat scones, vanilla cheesecake bites with blueberry compote, and cucumber finger sandwiches.

"From what Clara has told me," Patty said, leaning in. "Miles has been over there quite a bit."

Margie tossed an anxious look over her shoulder. "We shouldn't be talking about this. Annie is going to walk through that door any minute."

"We should ask her about it!" Patty said.

Margie shot her an admonishing look. "We should *not!* Poor Clara is suffering from wishful thinking. I am *telling* you, Miles Coleman will not be paired off. I have tried, and he was very clear that he would not be dating anyone until his daughter was out of the house. Or, really, not ever again."

It was nonsense. Margie even had a few friends who had asked about Miles for their daughters after seeing the ads. Margie assured them it was a worthless case.

Sheila lifted her teacup to her lips. "Maybe he just didn't like the women you were trying to set him up with."

Margie let out a huff. "I set him up with perfectly lovely women. He didn't object to *them*, he objected to the concept of romance in general. You know I'm not one to take no for an answer, but I have taken his *No* very seriously!"

Patty and Sheila looked at each other and smiled.

"I know everyone has gone crazy after seeing those dating ads with him in his firefighter getup," Margie continued, "but if you encourage Clara—or worse, Annie—you're going to break Annie's heart all over again."

"We can't have that." Sheila's expression turned serious. She turned to Patty. "You'd better keep your opinions to yourself."

"It's not an opinion. I'm merely reporting the facts," Patty said, taking a bite of vanilla cheesecake, her tone light and airy.

Sheila watched her for a moment before clearing her throat. "In other news, Lottie has been taking day trips with her mom."

Margie set her teacup down. She was eager to change the subject. "Has she! But she always comes back at night?"

It was funny to talk about her like an old friend. Lottie was an orca whom Sheila's father had helped capture many decades ago. In a twist of fate, Sheila's now-boyfriend Russell had owned a partial stake in the amusement park that housed

Lottie. Together, they'd worked to release her to a sea pen next to a neighboring island. Lottie was welcomed back into the family with open arms – or open fins.

"She does," Sheila nodded. "I guess she's not ready to say goodbye to her human friends yet. But she seems happy."

Margie caught a glint of something on Sheila's finger. "Hang on. What is that?" She rose to her feet. "Sheila! What is that?!"

A smile spread across Sheila's face. "I was wondering how long it would take you to notice."

Margie let out a shriek. "Is this an engagement ring?"

Sheila nodded. "It is. Russell popped the question last night."

"Congratulations!" Margie said, pulling her into a hug.

A jingle rang out, and the front door opened, letting a gust of cold air disturb the pleasantly warm space.

Margie lowered her eyes. "Not a peep about you know who."

Patty's placid smile shined back at her. "I don't know what you're talking about."

"Hello!" Annie called out.

Margie stood from her seat, popping her head out of the tearoom. "Hi, Annie!"

Annie pulled off her coat, her cheeks rosy with exertion. "Sorry I'm late. Bella came to watch the kids, and they were so happy to see her that I tidied up some last-minute things that I've been trying to get to all week."

Margie beamed. Introducing Bella and Annie might've been the best thing she'd done all year. The two of them got on like peas in a pod. Bella was thrilled about her new skills in babysitting, and Annie had help without a side of guilt.

On Margie's suggestion, Annie had asked her ex-husband to cover the cost of babysitting. Annie was surprised when he agreed without hesitation, the relief evident on her face when she broke the news.

Margie stayed silent. She knew Roy would agree to it. He wasn't a total monster, and he knew he was shirking his responsibilities. If an inexpensive teenage babysitter let him put off examining that for a bit longer, all the better.

"You don't have to explain yourself to us," Margie said, waving a hand. "We haven't really started. Just pouring the tea now."

"Great!" Annie said brightly.

She wasn't going to make Annie play the same game she had. Margie grabbed Sheila's hand and thrust it forward. "Look at this!"

Annie squealed, and after offering congratulations and exchanging some wedding planning talk, they all took their seats.

Margie sat back and watched Patty and Sheila's faces. There was no sign of them pushing topics they weren't supposed to push.

Could she trust them? Couldn't they see how much Annie had improved? Her hair was done, all shiny and bouncy. There was color in her face again, her complexion recovered from the ashen shade she'd sported in the summer. She was even wearing a stylish pair of wide-legged jeans everyone was doing now, and a flattering striped top.

"Is that new?" Margie asked, brushing a hand against her arm.

Annie nodded. "Yes, the whole outfit is new! I took a chance and bought a few things from an online clearance sale."

"You look adorable," Patty said.

"You seem energized," Sheila said with a smile.

Margie poured a cup of tea and pushed it toward Annie.

"Thank you." She accepted it with a smile. "I feel energized. I've been thinking a lot about this fundraiser. I've reached out to some local vendors, and they're willing to donate their services for a silent auction."

"That is a wonderful idea," Margie said.

She couldn't keep the smile off her face. *This* was the Annie she'd wanted to bring back—a woman full of life, full of joy. Yes, still a little tired around the eyes, but not the self-questioning, unmoored woman she had been when she'd gone through her divorce.

Annie didn't like to talk about it, but Margie knew that pain all too well. When her own husband had left her, her children were grown. But she knew the shock of it—losing not just an identity, but a future. Questioning everything.

It meant the world to Margie that Annie wasn't going through it alone. She deserved to know she belonged, that she was valued. That she mattered.

Annie pulled out a printed spreadsheet with yellow and pink highlights dashed all over. "Here are some of the companies donating and the values of their donation."

Margie snapped herself to attention, and they spent the next two hours planning the fundraiser and laughing over the endless treats Patty carried out from the kitchen.

She hadn't seen Annie relax like this in ages. She was laughing—*really* laughing. Thankfully, no one brought up Miles, just as Margie had asked.

Until Annie did.

"What was Bella's mom like?" Annie asked, seemingly out of the blue.

"That was before my time," Margie said quickly, hoping to change the subject.

But Patty took the bait. "Madeline was a lot like Bella. Feisty, funny, sharp as a tack. I'm not surprised that Miles never remarried."

A slight smile crossed Annie's face. "He's had his hands full."

"That," Patty said, "and he was waiting for someone as wonderful as Madeline."

The muscles in Margie's shoulders tensed. Did Annie catch that? *Was* waiting? As if his waiting was over?

Patty needed to put her theory to rest before it ruined Annie. Maybe Margie had agreed with her ever so slightly a few weeks ago, but now, after seeing how much happier and more whole Annie was, nothing was worth risking it.

"Patty," Margie said loudly, "you will have to give me the recipe for these apple scones. Hank would love them."

"Of course," Patty replied, betraying nothing in her gaze. She slowly stood from her chair. "I'll fetch it now."

Margie snuck a glance at Annie, but if she had any more questions, she kept them to herself.

It was best that way. If Annie was open to dating, Margie knew a handful of eligible bachelors. She could introduce them at the fundraiser, but she was not going to allow Annie to get a taste of the dressing down Miles could deliver.

Sixteen

By the end of Miles' post-holiday shift, his nerves were at their limit. They'd had a slew of nuisance calls – a woman who phoned at 3 AM to be transported to the hospital for a toe that had started hurting a month ago; a motor vehicle collision involving speeding and alcohol; and a man who called pretending he smelled gas.

"Look!" the man said, banging on his neighbor's door after they'd arrived. "Whatever you're cooking smells so bad that the fire department thought it was a gas leak!"

Normally, Miles was able to roll his eyes at these things and be grateful no one was hurt, but by the end of his forty-eight-hour shift, he'd lost all perspective. Even his coworkers were annoying him, and he was anxious to leave.

At shift change, he gathered his stuff, ignoring a new poster of his dating ad taped to the wall, and headed for the door.

"I hope your mood improves when you find love," Sam called after him.

Miles sighed. "Thanks."

Looking for love. What a joke. He'd had exactly zero interest in finding love in the last fourteen years. None. Never.

Except...whatever was happening when he saw Annie. Miles didn't know what was wrong with him. When it came to

Annie, he was like a man possessed. The entirety of his extensive Thanksgiving plan was to delight her, and when he saw how happy she was, he couldn't stop.

He was addicted to making her laugh. Beyond that, he felt an urge to get closer to her, to feel her in his arms.

Then he'd contrived a reason to do it. The dance.

It had crossed a line. It was completely inappropriate. But when he'd pulled her close, her body almost resting on his, the delicate notes of her perfume flooding his senses – he could feel in his bones that her problems would be forgotten if she'd only rest her head on his shoulder.

It was intoxicating. Maddening. It had taken everything in him not to pull her closer, envelop her in his arms and kiss her.

Thank goodness Bella had come home when she did. It had knocked some sense back into him.

If Bella had seen them dancing so closely, she would've known then and there that he was the biggest hypocrite on the island.

He'd told her for *years* that he wouldn't date. That he had no interest. No time. Yet she would've seen him close to another woman, in their own house, no less.

How hurt would Bella be? How much more of a joke would Miles be to her?

It wouldn't do. It didn't matter what had possessed him to act like a maniac with Annie. He had to gain control of himself. He needed to stop.

He pulled the door to the fire station open and paused. A white envelope sat on the ground, wet and dirtied at the edges. Had the mailman dropped it?

Miles stooped to pick it up, turning it in his hands. There was no postage, no address listed. The front had only the words "To the Firemen" written in black sharpie.

He ripped it open and pulled out a single, folded page inside. More black sharpie.

"KEEP PUSHING AND YOU WILL HAVE MORE FIRES YOU CAN'T PUT OUT!"

He sighed, his shoulders dropping. Though it was tempting to throw the note away and tell no one about its discovery, it would be unwise.

Miles turned and walked back into the fire station, yelling, "Guys, we got a live one!"

•　•　•

He didn't get a chance to talk to Bella until the next evening.

She was on her way out the door. "Sorry, Dad, I can't talk. I'm headed to Annie's."

He frowned. "Babysitting again?"

"No, she invited me for dinner. You're invited too!"

Miles took a step back, shaking his head. "That's all right."

When Bella was younger, he'd always had someone at the house with her when he worked a long shift. Now she took off on her own. The house was just... empty.

Truth be told, he felt empty. It was like she had no need for him. He just stood around in the house like an oaf, wondering when she'd be home.

"Don't be like that," Bella said with a sigh. "I'm sorry I yelled at you about giving me independence. This is different. I want you to come."

"You don't have to feel obligated to invite me," he said.

Bella had told him in no uncertain terms to stop showing up when she was babysitting, and he respected that. In this instance, however, he needed to stay away from Annie.

Her shoulders dropped. "I feel bad imagining you sitting at home by yourself."

A smile tugged on his lips. "You feel bad? For me? Your old dad?"

"I feel bad for you all the time." She paused. "You're pathetic."

A laugh burst out of him, and her face cracked in a smile. Her skill at sarcasm had always surprised him. She was so like her mom. So sharp. So funny.

"All right." He grabbed his coat. "We can't have that, then."

They walked down the road together, chatting. Miles told himself it would be fine. He'd talked to Annie about not sending Bella the wrong message, and she had understood. She hadn't reached out to him at all since Thanksgiving.

His heart sunk. Why hadn't she reached out to him? Couldn't they still be friends?

He was about to find out.

Bella climbed the stairs and opened the door without knocking.

That was quite familiar.

Miles followed as Clara welcomed them in. "Miles! I thought I saw you out there admiring your new handrail."

"Not admiring, I wouldn't say. Eyeing critically." He shook his head. "It's not the best-looking handrail I've ever seen."

She waved a hand. "Nonsense. It's art!"

Miles stripped off his jacket. The house was cozy and warm, cinnamon wafting in the air.

He cast a stiff look around. Annie was nowhere to be seen. Maybe she was avoiding him – though that would be hard to do in her own house. Maybe he shouldn't have come.

"How are you?" Miles asked.

"I'm feeling well, except my daughter keeps talking about leaving me and running off to the city."

"But you can't move!" Bella yelled out. "You're my mentor and I'll miss the kids too much!"

Annie emerged from the kitchen. Her hair was tied back with a few wisps free, making her look like a windswept goddess. He held his breath.

"You can always come and visit." Annie said. She caught Miles' eye and stopped abruptly. "Miles. Hi. How are you?"

He nodded a hello. "Doing well. How are you?"

"Things are bad!" Clara interrupted. "Annie is over here talking about moving to the mainland after Christmas!"

"So soon?" he blurted out, despite himself.

She looked down, picking a toy off the floor. "I've been trying to coordinate the Christmas handoff. Roy gets the kids for Christmas, and it's making me realize how hard it's going to be to do this forever. Plus, I got a call from a daycare where we were waitlisted. The others are all two or more years. They said I could take a tour and they might have an opening."

"It's bad enough we won't have the kids here on Christmas day," Clara said glumly. "Now you don't want them here at all!"

"It's embarrassing that I had to move in with my mother," Annie said sharply. "Roy is right. I need to strike it out on my own."

The topic ended as quickly as it started, with Annie picking up both twins and hauling them to the dinner table. They were in a wild mood, throwing food and laughing maniacally until the end of the meal.

It was only after they were done, when Miles was helping Annie clean up, that they had a moment alone.

"I don't like you talking like that," he said.

"Like what?" she asked, cocking her head to the side.

"Saying Roy is right." He shook his shoulders in a fake shudder.

Annie laughed. "He is, though. I know my mom's here, and she's a big help, but I should be able to do it on my own."

"There are no *shoulds* in single parenting. Believe me, I have experience. Let all the *shoulds* go and focus on reality."

She set a dish down, putting a hand to her forehead. "It's not that easy."

"Of course it's not easy," he said. "Being a single parent is impossibly hard. Why make it harder for yourself?"

"Because they need to see their dad. I'm making it harder by being here."

Miles sucked in a breath. As though Roy wasn't the one who had moved away. As though he was the one who had requirements as to when he'd see his children.

Nothing could have kept Miles from Bella after she was born. He would have moved heaven and earth to be with her.

"You're not the one making it harder," he said.

She shook her head.

He softened his tone. "Annie. He is living the life he wants to live. Don't forget that. What do *you* want?"

She was quiet for a beat, but when she looked at him again, her eyes were misty. "I don't know. I get jumbled, thinking about it. I think it's the fact that they won't be here for Christmas. It'll be my first Christmas alone."

That urge to sweep her up in his arms overtook him again.

He settled for putting his hand on hers. "You won't be alone. You'll have us."

There was so much more he wanted to say. That she couldn't leave. That he couldn't imagine not having her nearby.

But all he could do was look at her, desperation in his eyes.

"You're sweet." She pulled her hand away, casting a glance down the hallway.

Of course, Bella was just down the hall, wrestling with the twins. He'd forgotten himself.

Again.

His heart beat against his chest with a sickly speed. It wouldn't take much to stop lying. To tell her the truth. Pull her close again, close enough to smell her perfume. Close enough to make a bad decision.

Miles took a step back and cleared his throat. "We're your friends. We're here for you, whether you like it or not."

She let out a laugh. "Thanks, Miles."

He turned back to the sink, coward that he was.

Seventeen

Friends. He couldn't make it any clearer what their relationship was.

Yet the moment he'd stepped into the room, she'd melted. Her muscles softened, the tension in her stomach released, and she turned into some form of putty.

Annie hadn't stopped thinking about him since they had parted ways on Thanksgiving night. She could still feel his arms around her, still see his face only inches from hers.

He was gorgeous, and kind, and thoughtful. It wasn't her fault she'd turned into a human puddle. That's all she was – human. Who was she to resist the famous island firefighter?

For him to show up at her house like this, defending and encouraging her – it only added to her confusion.

Maybe that alone was reason to leave the island: to escape her very first crush.

"I don't know if Bella told you, but we got a threat at the fire station," he said.

There was a smile on his face, but Annie didn't find it funny at all. A pit formed in her stomach. "What kind of threat?"

Miles rolled his eyes. "Something about if we keep pushing, there will be more fires we can't put out."

A frown pulled at her mouth. Before, she would've been hard-pressed to name anyone who didn't consider firemen allies, if not outright heroes.

Now, the image of Lauren laughing in her new Porsche drifted into her mind. How had she been so cavalier about the firefighters not having working fire engines? Why had she been on the side of the private equity company?

It was so bizarre, and Annie hadn't had time to properly think about it, but now...she had a nagging feeling it could be connected.

"Do you think it's related to the monopoly case?" Annie asked.

He paused, lines creasing his handsome face.

Annie stared at him, helpless to look away, wishing she could reach out and touch him...

"I hadn't thought about that, actually," he said. "The case was thrown out at the state level, but they're going after them in a different way. The announcement went out last week that it's going to be taken up by the federal courts."

"That seems...significant," Annie said.

She was already running a text through her head that she wanted to send to Lauren. Maybe she could get her to talk about it. She said she'd worked for the judge; maybe she knew what was going on?

Or worse. Maybe she was somehow involved.

The pit in her stomach grew deeper. Would Lauren really sink as low as to leave a threat?

The idea was dizzying.

He grunted, his eyes focusing back on her. "That's a good angle. I kind of brushed it off, but I'll bring that up to everyone. Not that there's anything we can do."

Unless there was something he could do. Maybe he knew something about Lauren? Maybe, if she told him what she knew, they could piece together the truth.

Yet it was nothing more than gossip. It might be a betrayal of her friend for nothing.

Well, not for nothing. Was Annie letting herself be jealous of Lauren again? Or was it something worse – being so desperate for Miles' attention that she'd throw her own friend under the bus?

"Hey, don't worry about it," he said softly. "I thought you'd find it funny. I didn't want to worry you."

Annie thought she'd kept her struggle internal. Apparently not. He'd noticed.

She forced a more jovial expression on her face. "I'm just thinking, that's all."

"I'm sure that, after the fundraiser, we'll have more money than we know what to do with," he said, his mouth tilting into a smile.

The melt started again, her insides turning to goo. Why did he smile at her like that? Didn't he know the effect he had on women?

Of course he knew. Bella kept showing up with evidence of women throwing themselves at him. And he just laughed, rolling his eyes. He had no time for it.

Annie didn't need to throw herself at him. She could maintain some of her dignity.

Maybe a little of it, at least.

"I wouldn't want anything to happen to you," she said.

His smile faded, his eyes searching hers for a thoughtful beat. "Don't worry. All hope isn't lost. I'm not easily flammable."

Annie laughed. "I'm glad to hear that."

. . .

That evening, after her guests had left and the kids were sound asleep, Annie had some time to herself. The kitchen was clean, and while she folded laundry, she reasoned she could tick through some things on her to do list.

Except the only thing she could think about was Miles. His smile, his laugh. His hand on hers.

She hadn't imagined it, had she?

It didn't matter. In the end, she was no different than the desperate women sending headshots. She happened to live closer to him than they did.

Well. Maybe she was slightly different. Those women didn't know Miles. They didn't know what an extraordinary father he was. They didn't know how he loved to cook, and they didn't get to see in real time how he was a brave, level-headed firefighter, able to face any task. They didn't know how handy he was or how good he looked with a tool belt hanging off his hips.

They didn't know how kind he was, either. In Annie's experience, good-looking men were the worst sort. They knew they were handsome, they knew things were easy for them, and instead of taking it with a grain of humility, they took it as evidence of their own superiority.

Not Miles. His kindness was real. It ran to his bones. He probably thought Annie was a loser, trying to move closer to her ex-husband, but he didn't say that. He encouraged her. Told her he supported her. Told her they were friends.

If she weren't so starved for his attention, she'd never let him hear about her dealings with Roy. It wasn't like she thought Roy was an exemplary father. She knew he was lazy. She knew he showed only occasional interest in Leon and Noel. It was just that she wanted to find some way, any way, to fix that.

Annie's heart ached for her babies. They deserved better. They deserved a father who *wanted* to see them, who made the effort to take the ferry or the seaplane – whatever it took. They deserved a father who wanted to play with them and thought their babbling was as adorable as Annie did.

Yes, it was chaos and it was hard, but how could Roy miss all of it?

Her head was spinning again. Did she really believe Roy would be different if they lived closer to him? Or would their children always be a second thought? Would they grow up in that shadow, believing they didn't deserve more?

A sharp pain flashed in her chest. It felt like there was no solution. Obviously, if she'd married someone like Miles, this never would've been an issue, but it was too late for that. She thought she'd known Roy. They were high school sweethearts, for goodness sake, and he'd still turned out to be someone she didn't recognize.

She'd never understand it, but this was reality.

Was there any chance she could find someone like Miles, someone who would love them, *really* love them, as his own?

She'd heard stories. Stories of adoptions, or uncles raising their siblings' kids after tragedies, even dedicated stepfathers.

But it seemed impossible. She might as well wish for a magic genie to appear.

Even moving to Seattle seemed impossible. Every rental she'd found would take up most of her monthly salary. She was on a waitlist for eleven daycares, and most of them had told her it was hopeless unless she'd gotten on the list when she was first pregnant.

Still, that weekend, Margie and Sheila decided they were taking Annie dress shopping on the mainland, and she was going to tour the one daycare that said they might have space for them in two months.

Maybe she could find a higher paying job, she could move to Seattle, she could make it work. The twins would see Roy more, they'd settle into a smooth routine.

Maybe not all hope was lost for her little family. Even if she had messed it up from the start.

Eighteen

He dumped a pile of blankets next to the overstuffed picnic basket. They were ready for a night of stargazing. Miles could not wait to take Bella out to the beach. It was going to be a clear, albeit cold, night, and supposedly the best meteor shower of the year.

"Are you ready?" he yelled.

He stood in the kitchen, screwing the lid onto the thermos of hot chocolate he'd just made. A thermos of soup was already in the basket, along with sandwiches and cookies.

Bella came downstairs in a pink, shifty dress that hit above her knee.

Miles did a double take. "You're going to freeze in that."

Bella stared at him for a beat. "I have good news, and bad news, and more good news."

It slowly dawned on him that Bella was not dressed for stargazing.

"What's the bad news?" he asked wearily.

"The bad news is I can't go with you tonight."

He tossed the hot chocolate into the pile of blankets. "Okay," he said slowly. "What's up?"

"That's the good news! You know Olivia? That girl I told you about from my English class?"

"Yes..." he said, trying to recall all the information she'd told him about Olivia. "You're trying to get her to join the babysitters club."

Bella waved a hand. "Oh no, she was joking about joining. But she does have this big group of friends who watch old movies together, and I didn't think they were going to invite me, but they did. And it's tonight – we're watching *Casablanca* and going out for dinner after."

"*Casablanca*," he repeated.

This wasn't what he had expected, but how long had Miles really thought his daughter would want to spend her Saturday nights with him?

He didn't want to make her feel guilty, nor make her feel like she had to hang out with her pathetic old dad.

"Are you mad?" she asked, face tense.

"No, of course not!" he said cheerfully. "That sounds like fun. We'll catch the next meteor shower," he said, reaching to unpack the picnic basket.

"I have more good news, though," Bella said brightly. "I called Annie and told her we were going stargazing. She said she'd love to come."

Miles laughed. "Yeah, okay."

"I'm serious! So you can still go," she said. "I know you were really looking forward to it."

He set the hot chocolate thermos on the table, carefully weighing his words. "I was looking forward to going with you. I don't need a replacement."

Bella groaned. "Don't make me feel bad, Dad."

"I'm not trying to make you feel bad. You don't need to feel responsible to find a stand-in."

Especially not one that he couldn't stop thinking about.

"She's not a stand-in. I'm sure she's bored, too."

That seemed unlikely, and it was inappropriate. "I don't think Annie would want to go with me anyway."

Bella cocked her head to the side. "Why not? She sounded excited about it. She said her mom could watch the kids."

He was going to have to spell it out for her. "She's going to think," he said slowly, "that I'm trying to take her on a date or something."

A laugh burst out of Bella and she covered her mouth. "Yeah right! You're *way* too old for her."

He snapped his head back, an astonished smile on his face. "What's that supposed to mean?"

"Aren't you like, I don't know, fifteen years older than Annie? Her kids are just babies, and your kid is almost an adult."

Miles covered his mouth, laughing. "Hang on. Almost an adult?"

She drew herself up to her full height. "Indeed." Bella bowed her head slightly. "I'm practically grown."

He wasn't going to address that any further. "Did you know people can have kids at different times in their lives?"

Bella paused, seemingly pondering this.

"I think she's only three years younger than me," Miles continued.

That was a lie. He *knew* she was three years younger than him, because he'd looked her up online and read about her job and accidentally stumbled on her old wedding registry with Roy.

Bella frowned. "Oh. She looks younger than you."

"So not only have you insulted me," Miles said, crossing his arms, "now you're implying that I'm basically a grandpa."

"But are you mad?" Bella asked. "I just really can't believe they invited me and – "

"Of course I'm not mad," Miles said. "Please, go and have fun. Do you need a ride?"

She shook her head. "Um, no. Noah is coming to pick me up."

The muscles in Miles' back stiffened.

"Noah," he repeated.

"Yeah, I think I've mentioned him before. He's, like, part of this group, and he just got his license, so he said he'd pick me up."

A boy. An *older* boy, who had just gotten his license? So he could barely drive?

There were a million things he wanted to say, but Miles was at a complete loss as to what the *right* thing to say was.

He took a deep breath. "Is this Noah a safe driver?"

A smile lit her face. "Yes, the safest!"

Miles didn't care about the stargazing. The Annie bit had given him whiplash, but really, Bella wasn't focused on that at all. She was trying to make him happy, which made him feel guilty, all while she wanted desperately to be included by these new friends.

And now, a boy had entered the picture.

Everything all at once, as they say.

Trying to keep his expression carefree and bright was like performing surgery on himself. Awake. An amputation, maybe.

"Okay then, I trust you to make good choices," he said, falling back on a default phrase. "Don't stay out too late!"

"I won't!" she said, running and planting a kiss on his cheek.

Fifteen minutes later, Noah pulled up in an old minivan. He had the decency to get out of the car, walk up to the door, and ring the doorbell.

Bella rushed to beat Miles there, already wearing her coat. "Bye, Dad!" was all she said.

He stood behind her, dummy that he was, and waved, "Have a good night."

The door shut, and he was left to the silence.

Miles let out a sigh. There wasn't time to think through what had just happened, despite the sickly feeling in his chest. He had to undo whatever Bella had done with Annie.

What was that about Annie being too young for him? Nonsense.

Then again, how old were the women Bella had been showing him? He hadn't really paid attention. Thinking on it, the one she'd been pushing recently listed that she had "grown children." Maybe she was a grandma.

He wasn't *that* old yet. He still had some life in him.

Miles picked up the phone and dialed Annie's number. She answered with a bright, "Hey! I'm just getting ready now. But I can hurry it up if we're going to miss the meteor shower."

She was excited. He didn't want to spoil it for her, but he had to. "I hate to be the bearer of bad news, but Bella has ditched us. She's been picked up by an older boy named Noah."

A laugh burst out of Annie. "Oh no! Are you okay, Miles? Do you need to talk about it?"

He rubbed the back of his neck. The sick feeling hadn't gone away. "I think I do. It all happened so fast. I think I'm still in shock."

She laughed again. "I understand if you want to cancel. You know, if you need a night to recover."

He grinned into the phone. It was like Annie had read his mind.

Then again, what was the point of sitting at home and being sad when he could be outside being sad?

With her?

"We should go," he said, "if you're still interested."

"I can't wait! I've never seen a meteor shower."

"Really?" He cast a look at the picnic basket and blankets he'd packed. From this view, it was altogether a more romantic gesture than he'd anticipated.

It was too late to back out now, though. Especially if Bella now realized Annie was a viable candidate for her fantasy step-mother. She'd either try to force them together, or she'd realize that a real, live person was involved and suddenly change her mind about the whole thing.

Either way, it was probably his last chance to spend time with Annie unencumbered.

"Let me know when you're ready and I'll come and pick you up," he said.

"I should be ready in about fifteen minutes."

It was going to be far too romantic. He shouldn't do it. He knew that. He should cancel, then sit and stare at the clock until Bella came home.

He should, but he wouldn't.

Miles cleared his throat. "I'll see you then."

Following Noah's lead, when it was time to pick Annie up, he got out of his car and softly knocked on the door.

Annie emerged from the house wrapped in a long jacket and a cream-colored hat on her head, her hair peeking out at the bottom and sides.

She looked like an adorable Christmas card. Not that he could tell her that.

"I have a blanket," she said, motioning to the bundle tucked under her arm. "I don't know if it'll be warm enough, though, if it's windy wherever we're going."

"I've got a couple blankets, too. And hot chocolate and soup—all the hot things."

Annie smiled. "Seems like we'll be set then."

The entirety of their drive to South Beach was occupied with Miles talking about himself—the shock he felt when Bella not only canceled on him, but slyly told him she was going out with a boy.

"She is that age," Annie said thoughtfully.

"She's too young. Doesn't she seem young?" Miles countered. "I think it was only two Christmases ago I was buying her Barbies."

"Did you buy her a Ken doll, too?" Annie asked with a smile.

He sighed. "That was where I went wrong, isn't it?"

"You didn't go wrong anywhere," Annie said, casting him a sympathetic smile. "It's a great sign that she told you about Noah. She's not hiding things from you, even if she feels sheepish about it all."

Sheepish. That was how Bella had acted, wasn't it? The uneasy feeling in his chest quieted. She had been excited, he'd noticed that, but she also felt a bit embarrassed. Perhaps this wasn't the bold leap into adulthood he'd imagined.

It was a small comfort. Annie was always a comfort.

They parked the car and to his surprise, no one else was there—usually at least one or two other families went out for the meteor showers, especially on a clear night like this. Maybe the cold weather was keeping people away, but Miles didn't feel cold at all. He was so hot he wanted to take off his jacket, heat pulsing out from his chest. It seemed to get worse whenever he looked at Annie.

They found a suitable spot on the beach and Miles laid the blanket on the ground.

"I would start a fire," he said. "But we're in a fire ban."

"I know," she said. "I checked. The fire danger is 'very high.'"

He shot her a look. "I'm impressed you keep up with our warnings."

"I always heed the fire department," she said solemnly, taking a seat on the blanket.

He sat down next to her, their legs nearly touching, and pulled out a second blanket to cover themselves with.

Annie shivered, and without thinking, he scooted closer to her. She cast him a fleeting smile.

The intimacy of the moment was palpable, and Miles knew no way to deal with the tension other than offering food and drink.

"I have lentil soup," he said, reaching over her to open the picnic basket, "and hot chocolate. Anything sound good right now?"

"I'll try the soup," she said, hands clasped beneath the blanket.

He pulled out a thermos for her and poured a serving into the lid. Annie's shoulders were tense, her posture huddled.

"This should help," he said, handing it to her.

"Thanks." She took a sip. "Oh wow. This is delicious. Did you make this?"

He nodded and poured a small amount from his thermos as well, heat still pumping from his chest.

"It's one of Bella's favorites," Miles said. "The soup."

"Ah. It's very good." She sat, head tilted up to him. "You're a great dad, you know."

She seemed to mean it.

He realized he was scowling at her and softened his expression. "Thanks. It doesn't always feel that way." Miles paused. "I guess I just didn't expect her to grow up *that* fast. I know everyone says it happens in the blink of an eye, but it's still so easy to miss."

"It's because it's not one blink of an eye. It's thousands. Thousands of moments you realize they've grown up, and the old version of them is gone forever."

"Yeah. Man, that's the truth." Miles shook his head. "You're a great mom too, you know."

She cast him a wry smile. "I wasn't fishing for compliments. I'm a mess."

"You're not a mess," he said firmly.

"I'm a mess," she reiterated. "I spend half of my time feeling sappy about them getting older, then the other half wishing away the difficult times – the tantrums, the night wake ups, the moods. And all the time feeling guilty."

"Sounds like a great mom to me." He turned so he was facing her. "You're in the thick of it."

"Yeah," she said softly. Annie kept her eyes fixed upward. "I already see so many stars."

He stared at her, the gentle slope of her nose, the delicate eyelashes, her beautiful round eyes twinkling with starlight.

Did she really feel that way? A mess? He wished she could see herself how he saw her. Bold, determined. Endlessly kind in the face of so much unfairness.

"I've never seen this many stars in my life," she whispered.

It was hard to look away from her, the wonderment and delight obvious on her face.

He tore his eyes away and looked up, the sky littered with light. The Milky Way glowed above them, but he didn't have much interest in stargazing tonight.

"I don't see any meteors yet," she added, squinting. "Should I have a wish ready for when I see one?"

"Yes. Keep watching," he said. "Have lots of wishes."

"I just have one," she said softly.

His heart leapt, and he glanced down at her. In this moment, he only had one, too, though he doubted their wishes were the same.

Miles forced himself to look away from her.

"Each meteor puts on its own show," he said. "They come as streaks of light, some bright, some faint. They've been traveling for millions of years, only to catch fire as they enter earth's atmosphere."

She gasped. "I see one! There!"

He caught himself staring at her again, this time at her lips. He tried to follow the path of her finger, but he saw nothing.

"I can't believe how quiet it is. There's no sound at all!" she said breathlessly.

He took the empty cup of soup out of her hands and set it down. "Here," he said. "You can lay down. You'll be warmer, and you won't miss any meteors."

She laid back, pulling the blanket to her chin. "Oh, I like this very much," she said, grinning.

Miles laughed, hesitating. It took everything he had not to reach out and brush the errant strand of hair out of her eyes. His stare lingered a moment too long, and she caught his eye, a puzzled look on her face.

He quickly settled in beside her, his shoulder touching hers. He didn't say anything about it, and neither did she.

"Another one!" Annie said with a gasp.

This time, Miles saw it, too, an exceptionally bright fireball across the sky, its trail lingering for a few seconds after it blasted apart.

"Incredible," Annie whispered.

"Yeah," he said, adding a silent, "You are."

Nineteen

"I was a mess, too," Miles said. "Especially when Bella was little. It's so hard when they're small and people tell you to enjoy every moment. It only makes you feel more guilty when most of the time, you're barely surviving."

Annie turned her head to look at him. He was so close to her. So close she could almost kiss him. "Well, you were grieving, too."

"And you're not grieving?" He turned to her, scrunching up his beautiful face. "I know it's not the same, but you went through a divorce. You lost the person you thought Roy was, and you lost the life you thought you'd have."

It was no good looking into his eyes like this, especially when he looked into her mind like that.

She turned back to face the milky white sky above her. "Stop being so empathetic. You're going to make me spill my guts to you. *Again.*"

His laugh rang out, deep and long. "That's not my intention."

"Good." She didn't need to tell him about her problems. No one needed to hear the thoughts that swirled around in her head.

"You're allowed to talk about it, though. You should know that," he said.

She was silent for a long while, his words working past her defenses, past her excuses.

Finally, she said, "I don't have time to grieve that life."

The words hung between them. She looked over at him and he was propped up on one arm, watching her intently.

She went on. "It's Noel and Leon's lives I grieve. What type of family are they going to have? It doesn't escape me that Roy is not a dedicated father." A sigh hissed out of her, leaving her as deflated as she felt. "What type of dad did I pick for them?"

"That is not your fault," Miles said firmly. "None of us know what kind of parents we're going to be until we get there, let alone what kind of parents our partners will be."

"I feel like," she said slowly, "I should've known he was going to run for the hills. Somehow. There should've been a sign. I must have missed it."

He remained quiet, eyes intent on her. After a moment, he said, "I know I've told you this before, but there's a reason for the old joke about men leaving to get milk and never coming back. It's essentially what my dad did and—listen, I know it doesn't make a disappointing parent any less disappointing—but it's common. So common. And it's not your fault."

How heartbreaking that it was common, and that it had happened to Miles, and Noel, and Leon.

But if it was common, it meant people survived it, right?

Miles had survived it, and had gone on to be the most wonderful man on the planet.

Another meteor streaked across the sky. Her cheeks were frozen; her nose had to be bright red with cold, but she didn't care. She was witnessing a miracle in the quiet, expansive universe, and she was experiencing it with Miles.

"I saw that one," he said.

She looked over – his huge form lying next to her, his broad shoulders just touching hers, his chest rising and falling. What would it be like to lay her head on his chest, close her eyes, and drift to sleep? It would be the best rest she'd had in years.

"Why can't Roy be like you?" Annie said, then regretted it as soon as she said it.

"You mean what Bella would tell you is an overprotective, cloying nuisance?" Miles suggested.

Annie scoffed. "No, that's not you. Not at all. I'm sorry to inform you of this, but you're like the perfect dad."

He leaned in closer, their faces almost touching. "The perfect dad," he repeated with a laugh. "Tell me more about how perfect I am."

She lightly shoved his shoulder. He didn't move. "It's true. I'm embarrassed to even tell you about Roy. You must think he's a monster, and that I'm – "

"I can assure you, I'm not perfect. I don't always do what I should."

"Oh, you mean sometimes you run into the fire only ten times instead of eleven? That you only save the kittens and not the pet fish?"

"No." His voice was deep now, gravelly. "Sometimes I do things I know I shouldn't."

Her heart jumped.

He leaned in, his face closer to hers.

A wind blew, but Annie no longer felt the cold. The ocean hummed beside them, looping as though time were standing still.

She locked eyes with Miles, not daring to say the wrong thing. He was going to kiss her. She could feel it, the way he was looking at her, how close he'd gotten...

He pulled away, laying on his back, his hands behind his head.

"I don't think Roy is a monster." His voice was normal again. "I think he's depressingly average."

"Depressingly average," Annie repeated, laying back.

Way to misread the signs. Thankfully he couldn't see the burning in her cheeks, or the burning in her chest, either.

Man, she was bad at this. It was like she'd only ever kissed one man – because she had.

"I think you're extraordinary," he said.

Her mouth ticked up in a half smile. "Thanks."

"I mean it. I admire you in every way." He turned his head. "Every way."

Her heart leapt at the words. She'd told him he was the perfect dad. Somehow, he'd found something even nicer to say about her.

• • •

Annie spent the next few days replaying his words over and over. For once, she wasn't kicking herself for complimenting him. He deserved to hear it, especially considering what he'd said to her.

Admired her in *every* way. Did that mean physically, too? It seemed to affirm that he had almost kissed her. She couldn't have misread the situation *that* badly.

In that moment, her one wish had quickly turned to two. There were more than enough meteors to support two wishes: first, that her kids got the best father they could have out of Roy.

The second was that Miles would kiss her.

She knew he was not interested in a relationship. She knew he had turned down literally hundreds of women and he was the hottest man on the island – in every way.

It didn't matter to her. One kiss. It didn't have to mean anything; he didn't have to commit to her. She just wanted that feeling to last a moment longer – the way he made her feel. Seen. Worthy. Alive.

In her more crazed moments, she told herself she'd kiss him herself the next chance she had.

Of course, she knew she wouldn't.

That wish didn't have much chance of coming true, but her first wish – she could do something about that.

Emboldened by his assessment of Roy, Annie did what she had been avoiding for ages. She typed up an email to Roy about her visit to Seattle. She was polite but firm, telling him she had toured the only daycare available to them (leaving out the potentially embittered comment that he was free to get the kids onto waitlists, too, if he was so eager for them to move), she'd found it unacceptable, and she couldn't see herself moving the kids anytime in the near future, if at all. She cited the lack of appropriate childcare, the lack of help, and the affordability.

The money was a constant issue for her. She was sick of feeling like a sheepish teenager every time she asked him for money, justifying everything like it was her fault the twins had outgrown all their clothes, or needed to size up in diapers, or simply needed to eat three square meals a day.

In the end, she calculated the twins were with her roughly ninety-six percent of the time, and kept this in the back of her mind when she asked if he could please set up a scheduled money transfer of three hundred dollars a month to help her support them.

She hit send with Miles' words echoing in her head and his face hovering in her mind's eye.

Twenty

It was no good. Miles had come dangerously close to kissing Annie. Lying under the stars, watching the meteors burn, their voices hushed against the rolling waves, he'd almost set fire to his life.

It was far too cold outside, and it had allowed them to get far too intimate. What was he thinking?

At least he hadn't actually done it. He'd managed to stop himself, so that was good, right?

No. It wasn't just the almost-kiss. Anyone could excuse a kiss. The real problem was he was dangerously close to falling in love with her, and that was the last thing either of them needed.

Bella was clearly going through the challenges of adolescence. She needed her father to be steadfast and stable, not losing his head over the pretty neighbor down the road.

That same evening, she came home from her evening with Noah floating on a cloud. She didn't have much to share, but she was all smiles for the next week.

Miles was happy for her. Annie was right; it seemed innocent enough, and age-appropriate. Bella was the one who was supposed to be silly and getting pulled into puppy love. Not Miles.

Further, he knew how these things went. He had been a teenager once. On the horizon, on the other side of Bella's whirlwind first romance, was the most devastating heartbreak Bella would ever suffer.

It may not be this week or even this year, but it was inevitable. That first heartbreak cut the deepest, and Miles needed to be there for her when it struck.

Thinking of it, maybe that was what Annie was going through. Roy had been her high school sweetheart, after all. She had made no allusions to being experienced in the art of dating and love, and it was all the more reason to leave her alone.

That didn't mean avoiding her entirely, though. On Wednesday, he had the day off, and the subs for Bella's school band fundraiser arrived. His plan was to spend the day delivering the sandwiches to everyone who had ordered them, something he did every year.

Annie's order was last on his list. He figured she'd be at work, and he was right. When he knocked on the door, Clara appeared.

"Special delivery," he said, holding up a bag.

"Miles! What a welcome surprise," Clara said. She accepted the bag and peered inside. "Annie's at work today, at the outpost site."

He'd figured as much. It was for the best, despite the sinking in his chest. "I threw in an extra pepperoni roll. I wanted her to try it."

"That's sweet." Clara paused, slowly raising her eyes. "Come to think of it, Annie forgot to pack a lunch this morning. Well, *forgot* isn't the right word. She ran out of time, because Leon was running around yelling about using the potty before school."

"He used the potty?" Miles asked. "And he *said* potty, too?"

"He did!"

"That's amazing!" Miles said.

"Yeah." Clara's face spread into a warm smile. "Anyway, I won't keep you, but if you wanted to bring one of these sandwiches out to her, I know she'd be appreciative."

The load on his chest lightened. It wasn't like he sought out these chances to see her. They appeared, and like an addict, he couldn't resist them. It was chemical.

"I'd love to," he said, unable to keep a smile off his face.

Clara gave him the directions to the lab outpost and he made his drive to the west side of the island.

He'd never seen the building before. It was old and drab, almost abandoned-looking, standing alone with the backdrop of the sea.

He pulled into a spot next to Annie's car, the only one in the small gravel lot, and surveyed the building. It was three stories tall with ancient-looking windows and peeling eggshell paint. The roof was lopsided and the building itself looked misshapen.

Still, he liked it. It had that seaside charm that old buildings had, like it had been rocked by the waves but never knocked down.

Miles walked to the entrance and knocked on the door. Annie was already in the window, smiling at him.

"My mom texted to warn me you were coming," she said, ushering him in. "You really didn't have to do this."

"It's my pleasure. I've been delivering all over today, and when your mom said you were lunch-less because of a successful potty trip this morning, I thought we needed to celebrate."

Annie let out a groan. "Yeah, I feel bad now that I rushed him and he *actually* had to use the potty."

Her eyes were reddened, and her complexion was pale.

"Are you okay?" he asked.

"That obvious, huh?" she asked, casting her eyes down.

"I just know you well," he said, then immediately corrected himself. "I mean, I see you often and you don't..." Miles frowned. "There's no way to recover that statement, is there?"

Annie laughed. "I know what you mean. No offense taken. I know I'm a mess."

He let out a breath. "What's going on? Have you been feeling guilty about Leon all morning? I'm sure he's not dwelling on it."

"No, not that." She took a seat on a nearby swivel chair. "It's Roy."

The muscles in his jaw tightened. "Roy," he said in a low voice.

"All that stargazing went to my head. I got the idea I was shortchanging the twins by not expecting more from Roy, and that night I typed up an email telling him that I wanted him to regularly send money so they could have everything they need. I even attached a bunch of receipts from groceries, and diapers, doctors visit copays from being sick four times this winter already, and their winter coats I had to buy new because I couldn't find any hand-me-downs in time..."

Her voice trailed off. She buried her face in her hands.

Miles set the bag down before taking a seat next to her and touching her shoulder. "Sounds reasonable to me."

"Roy didn't think so." She looked up, biting her lip, measuring her words. "He said he's not going to fund my lavish lifestyle on a remote island, so I either move to Seattle or find a way to fund it myself."

The blood rose in Miles's throat, heat pulsing in his ears. "Did you remind him that he's the one who moved away?"

"I didn't respond yet. He said he's already paying for half of the daycare costs, and if I want child support, then I can take him to court. He said he'll be filing for primary custody." Her voice broke on the last word, a sob catching in her throat.

Miles dropped to his knees in front of her and took her hands in his. "Annie, listen to me. Please," he said.

She looked down at him, tears rimming her eyes. "It was stupid of me. I never would have done it if..."

"This is a page from the deadbeat dad handbook," Miles said. "Whenever they get called out about not wanting to pay to support their children, they always threaten to go for custody." He softened his tone. "It's not going to work."

She didn't respond, staring down and chewing her lip.

He spoke again. "How much did you ask for?"

"Three hundred dollars a month," she said. "Just enough to cover diapers and a little bit of the grocery bill. They're eating so much more now, and a lot gets wasted, but I still have to make the meals and – "

"Are you kidding me?" Miles had to suppress a scoff. "That's it?"

"I didn't want to ask for too much."

"That's nothing. Literally nothing." He shook his head. "How much does he make?"

"He was making two hundred and fifty thousand a year when we separated," Annie said.

Miles looked around the lab. "I'm guessing you are not making that much."

A weak smile formed on her lips. "I am not."

"If he's stupid enough to take you to court, he is going to owe you five times that. Easily."

She sucked in a breath. "I don't want the money. I'll find another way. If he gets full custody..."

"They are not going to award an absent father full custody," Miles said firmly.

"What if he can prove I'm not able to provide for them? Because I'm not."

"You've been providing just fine from what I can see," Miles said. He squeezed her hands, ignoring the fact that he shouldn't be holding them at all. "I'm not an attorney, but I've been talking to a lot of them recently, and I can tell you it's not going to look good that he left and hasn't spent any time with his kids before suddenly expressing his interest in having full custody."

Annie sighed. "Maybe."

If only he could sweep her up in his arms. If only he could convince her of how wonderful she was, how obvious it was to anyone who looked.

"No judge will take kindly the games he's trying to play. They've seen it all before," he said.

"I hope you're right. I just wish..." A tear spilled out and slipped down her cheek.

He stood and grabbed a tissue from her desk.

Annie dabbed at her eyes before speaking again, her voice clear and firm. "I wish I was stronger. I wish I was strong enough to get through all of this."

"You are strong enough, and you're not doing it alone."

Annie crumpled the tissue in her hand and peered up at him.

He went on. "You have all of us. Your mom, Margie, Sheila, Bella." He leaned in, his head tilted to hers. Did he dare say it? "Me."

"And Roy probably has a thousand-dollar-an-hour attorney."

Miles frowned. He probably did, and that wouldn't look good in front of the judge, either. "You know, last year Bella got in trouble for egging a bunch of houses. I don't condone that sort of behavior, but she was very good at it. Excellent aim. I don't mind sending her to the mainland, if you catch my drift."

The edge of her mouth tilted into a smile. "Eggs are too expensive. You can't waste them like that."

A laugh burst out of him. "You're right. We'll find something more economical."

She smiled, shaking her head. "Yeah."

His chest swelled. What he really wanted to do was offer to fly to the mainland, find Roy in his place of work, punch him in the face, and walk out.

He knew Annie wouldn't agree to it; he'd have to figure out where Roy worked on his own. Shouldn't be too hard...

"Thank you, Miles. It means a lot."

"Any time." He meant it.

She let out a breath and stood. "Would you like a tour of the lab? It's not the most exciting place, but we've got microscopes."

He smiled. There were a thousand things he wanted to do. Pull her close. Whisk her away. Hire an attorney for her. Pay for the winter coats himself.

But none of that was what Annie wanted. She didn't want to be rescued. She wanted a friend.

A friend, not a guy who kept hitting on her, who couldn't stop thinking about kissing her and taking her in his arms.

The last thing she wanted was another guy messing up her life. Miles was determined not to do that to her.

"I'd love a tour," he said.

Twenty-one

Christmas day. Annie surprised herself, sleeping in until eight o'clock, opening her eyes to the sun blasting through the window.

She couldn't remember the last time she'd awoken after sunrise. Rolling over to check her phone – nothing. No messages. No pictures of the twins opening their presents Christmas morning.

It wasn't unexpected. Roy had followed through on his threat to take her to court. He'd filed a motion for a parenting plan with the superior court, and their hearing was set in seven weeks. Of course he'd punish her on Christmas by making her wonder what they were doing. *How* they were doing.

The smell of coffee wafted in from the kitchen, pulling Annie out of bed. Her mom was already up, a red and white velvety Christmas hat atop her head.

"Merry Christmas, sweetheart," she said, kissing her on the cheek.

Annie poured herself a mug of coffee. "Merry Christmas, Mom."

Annie shuffled, pajama-clad, to the couch. Their small tabletop Christmas tree had two new presents beneath it. A small box wrapped in shining gold paper, and a much larger box wrapped in silver with red satin ribbon.

"What's this?" Annie asked.

"A little something for you," Clara said, settling in next to her.

"I thought we said no presents," Annie said.

"It's not *really* a present." Clara lifted the smaller of the two presents and placed it in Annie's hand. "The other one is from Margie and Sheila. Santa dropped it off."

Annie smiled at her. "Santa's working for Margie now, eh?"

She tore off the wrapping paper and revealed a dark violet, velvet box. Inside was a gold ring with a glittering sapphire surrounded by a dusting of little diamonds.

She looked up at her mom, her mouth hanging open. "Grandma's ring? I can't take this."

"Of course you can," she said, beaming. "It deserves to see the light of day again."

"It's too fancy for me to wear," Annie said, slipping it onto her ring finger. It fit perfectly, throwing flashes of colored light from the Christmas tree.

"You can wear it to the fundraiser," Clara said.

"Oh. Yeah." Annie looked up at her. "Thank you, Mom."

Clara beamed. "Open the big one!"

Annie eyed the package before picking it up. "I wish they hadn't gotten me anything."

"Oh hush," Clara said. "There's a card. Read that first."

Annie unfolded it and read aloud. "Annie, we wanted to get you something to thank you for not just the idea for the fundraiser, but for all the incredible work you've put into it. You deserve to shine. Love, Margie and Sheila."

She pressed her lips into a line, willing the tears to go away. It was going to be a weepy day.

"I can't wait to see," Clara said.

Annie cleared her throat and set the card down. She had a feeling she knew what it was.

She pulled on the silk ribbon and it came undone easily. Setting the box on the ground, she lifted the lid. A gasp escaped her.

It was a dress, nestled in a bed of tissue paper. It was *the* dress she'd tried on, at their insistence, the one that was laughably expensive.

She lifted the gown from the box, the sequined pink flowers shining in the morning sun. The rest of the dress was champagne gold, the perfect tone to warm her complexion. It had long sleeves, and a V-neckline that was probably too much for a mom of two, and a delicate pink embroidered waist.

It felt substantial in her hands, like the dress of someone far more important.

Clara sighed, clutching her hands to her chest. "Oh Annie, it's beautiful. Put it on!"

"I can't put it on! I'm a mess!" Annie pointed to the bun on the top of her head.

"You're right, you need to take a shower. Freshen up. Go on!"

Annie cast her mom a look, but she didn't protest. Without prompting, she'd wallow in flannel all day.

This dress deserved more than that. She carefully placed it back in the box, texted a hasty thank you to Margie and Sheila, then took her mom's advice.

Not ten minutes after showering and drying her hair, there was a knock at the front door. Annie rushed to open it, her heart pounding against her chest on the off chance that maybe, just maybe, Roy had decided to have a truce for the day and bring the twins around.

No such luck. She pulled the door open with too much force, cold wind blasting in. On the doorstep stood Miles and Bella, grinning.

"Hit it, Dad!"

Miles pressed a button on his phone as Jingle Bells started to play. Then they started singing.

"Dashing through the snow in a one-horse open sleigh..."

Annie covered her open mouth with her hands, laughter forcing its way out.

Miles went hard on some improvised *Ho Ho Ho*s, earning a sharp look from Bella, which he ignored.

Clara stood with her arm around Annie. "Noel would've loved this."

"I love this," she said through laughter.

When the song ended, Clara clapped loudly and called out, "Bravo!"

"Real life Christmas carolers!" Annie said, unable to contain her grin. "Do you want to pop inside, or are you hitting every house in the neighborhood?"

"I hope not," Bella said, stepping inside. "I don't know if you can hear, but he's tone deaf."

Miles scrunched his nose. "I'm not tone deaf. I sound great. We should make a firefighter Christmas album."

Bella rolled her eyes. "Don't even joke about that, Dad."

He shut the door, standing in front of it all wide-shouldered and hopelessly masculine, dressed in a red and black buffalo flannel, looking every bit the part of a Christmas album star.

Why did he always have to look so good?

"Merry Christmas," Annie managed to say.

"Merry Christmas," he said with a warm smile. "I am going to be presumptuous and assume you don't have any plans for the day."

Annie looked around the empty house. It was obvious, and Annie suspected her mom had told him the same. Her urge for Annie to shower made sense. "You would be right."

"Perfect. Then you won't mind us hanging out here before heading over to my buddy's farm for a sleigh ride later. You're both invited, of course."

"It's more of a farm cart being pulled by a horse," Bella said.

"There's still a horse," Miles countered. "And I'm going to bring hot chocolate."

Though staying home and weeping felt like the right thing to do, even Annie couldn't imagine turning down an opportunity to see Miles.

She glanced at her mom. "We can't say no to hot chocolate."

He smiled that stunning smile. "I was hoping you'd say that."

Her heart stopped. She blinked. "Would either of you like coffee or tea?"

"I'm allowed to have decaf coffee!" Bella announced.

Annie nodded. "Coming right up!"

Miles followed her into the kitchen. "I hope you don't mind us dropping in. Your mom said it would be okay."

"Not at all." She met his gaze, steady and calm. "It's nice to see you."

"How are you doing?" he asked.

She was quiet for a moment, listening to the kettle heating up. "Better now."

One side of his mouth tilted up.

"Is this a plant?" Bella yelled out. "My dad has been trying to get me to watch this for years."

Annie shot him a quizzical look before returning to the living room. Bella had a *National Lampoon's Christmas Vacation* DVD in her hand.

"It's not a plant," Annie said. "It's a great movie and we rewatch it every year."

She frowned. "It's older than I am. I am not watching a movie that's older than me."

Annie met Miles' eyes. He shook his head as if to say, "Here we go again."

"What if," Annie said, kneeling in front of the TV, "as a Christmas gift to me, we all watch it together?"

Bella stared at her, arms crossed over her chest. Finally, she let out a sigh and said, "All right. For you, Annie. But only you."

After popping some popcorn, they settled into their seats. Bella piled pillows on the floor and insisted on stretching out on them. Clara sat next to Annie, and Miles positioned himself at the other end of the couch. It was foolish of her, but Annie had wanted him to sit next to her. To maybe get the chance for their legs to brush against one another, to feel the sparks zinging up her leg.

After he had surprised her in the lab, she found herself thinking about all the times he'd been so close, yet still so far from her. Laying next to her on the blanket, grasping both of her hands when he offered to have Roy's house egged.

There was a steadiness to him. It was in his even moods, in his soothing presence. More than that, she felt it even when he wasn't there. It was like his calm voice had invaded her head. She could hear him telling her things would be okay.

Oddest of all, she believed him. Maybe she was naive, but to her, he was a real-life hero.

Foolish indeed.

The movie started, and much to her teenage chagrin, Bella kept laughing.

"These people are nuts," she said.

"They're family," Miles said simply. "All families are nuts."

"And they make us nuts," Clara added, chuckling at her own joke.

Miles and Annie exchanged wary looks before bursting into laughter themselves.

When the movie was done, Bella admitted it was enjoyable, and possibly even a classic. Then, they loaded into Miles' truck and made the drive to the farm.

On the way there, Annie's phone lit up with a text message from Roy's dad, of all people.

He had always been a pleasant man, easy to joke and offer a smile. He was friendly to Annie, but completely overshadowed by his wife and silent since the divorce.

Her heart thudded as she opened the message. Had something happened to the twins? Did she need to fly to the hospital?

But no. It was pictures he had taken of Leon and Noel opening presents, playing with toys, and eating cookies. There were smiles on their faces and icing on the Christmas outfits she'd bought for them.

They were okay. They were having a good time, even.

She tucked her phone away, hiding the happy tears in her eyes, as they got to the farm. There were two other families there, both with school-aged kids. Miles introduced them and they stood around a propane fire (allowed, per Miles), sipping on hot chocolate as the kids tried to roast marshmallows.

Miles' friend swung by with his horse and carriage, welcoming the first load of riders onboard. The kids leapt up, Bella included.

When they returned, Miles asked Annie if she was ready to try it out.

"I'd love to," she said.

Her mom started after them, but stopped herself. "That'll make my hip too stiff, actually," she said, returning to the fire.

It was just the two of them, then. Annie's heart leapt as Miles slid in next to her.

"I hope you don't mind," he said. "At the very least, I can keep you warm."

The day had been far too magical – from the surprise pictures and gifts, to the caroling, to getting to watch an old favorite through Bella's eyes.

It had all been because of him. Well, mostly because of him. Always there for her to fall back on.

Their sleigh pulled away with a start, and something like the Christmas spirit overcame her. She squeezed his hand.

"Thank you, Miles. For everything. You've rescued my Christmas. I thought I'd be sitting and crying into my hot chocolate."

"My pleasure," he said.

"I'd always pick a spot next to you, and not just because you're warmer than everyone else." She stretched and planted a kiss on his cheek.

His eyes flashed wide, red filling in his cheeks.

He looked down at her, his face split by a wide smile. "Best gift I've gotten all day," he said.

Annie laughed, her chest glowing with boldness. She laid her head on his shoulder and they passed the rest of the ride side by side, not saying a word.

Twenty-two

It was hard not to read into it – the closeness on the sleigh ride, the relaxed weight of Annie leaning into him.

The kiss.

Yeah, it was just a kiss on the cheek. It didn't mean anything. Miles knew that. It was how she might kiss an elderly relative, or Santa Claus.

Most likely Santa Claus. Wasn't that how he'd acted? He'd even worn a hat. She thought she'd have a terrible Christmas, and because of his butting in, she'd had a decent Christmas. Rescued, as she put it.

There was nothing romantic to the kiss, and he wasn't going to let his mind wander down that road. Annie didn't need him pining after her.

He didn't need to pine after her, either. It was bad enough that he thought only of how to see her again and again. Imagining some scenario where a cheek kiss meant she was interested in him wouldn't help anyone.

After the holiday, everything went back to normal. The twins returned from the mainland, with Roy failing to set up another exchange date, the court date looming in the distance. Bella kept babysitting, and Miles kept whipping up dinners for both families to enjoy together.

The only addition to their routine was a weekly movie night with Bella. They rotated picks, with Bella selecting Korean dramas, and Annie and Miles dusting off movies from their childhood.

Bella relented to watching the "oldies," as she called them, and gave a rating via the traditional thumbs-up and thumbs-down system. So far, she approved of the *Back to the Future* movies, but gave Annie's beloved *Clueless* two thumbs down for "rampant misogyny and embarrassing clichés."

"Kids are tough these days," Annie murmured after Bella left the room.

"You have no idea," Miles said. "I still think it's a cute movie, though."

"Me too!" she whispered. "I told her it's loosely based on Jane Austen's *Emma,* but she wasn't impressed."

"That Paul Rudd, though," Miles said, shaking his head. "What a hunk."

Annie suppressed a smile. "Stop it."

"I'm serious. He's a beautiful man. Funny, too. A total package."

Annie sighed. "Don't let Bella hear you say that. I'm sure there's a word for what you're saying, and it wouldn't be good."

"Wouldn't dream of it."

The weeks went on, perfect and comfortable, without any hints of romantic feelings from Annie. They enjoyed one another's company, and the fact that she kept him at arm's length, as a *friend,* made it easier – easier to pretend, at least.

He could pretend he was happy with just friendship. He could pretend the urge to pull her into his arms didn't flare every time he saw her. He could pretend his mind didn't drift off when she spoke, imagining what it would be like to finally press his lips to hers...

Miles' job was to pretend to be a sane person when he felt wildly insane.

All things considered, it was going pretty well.

One bright Saturday morning in February, Bella woke him early. "I have a surprise, and you have to promise you won't be mad," she said.

He looked at her, bleary-eyed from his pillow. "Is it breakfast in bed? I won't be mad about that. Bring it in."

She bit her lip. "No, but that would have been a good way to soften the blow."

He sat up, yawning and stretching. "It's never too late for breakfast."

"No, it's too late." She shook her head. "We need to go. I need you to pick someone up from the ferry."

His eyebrows shot up. "Is something wrong?"

"You have to promise you won't be mad," she repeated.

If she was in some kind of trouble.

He sat up. "Of course I won't be mad. What's going on?"

"Good." A smile flashed across her face. "I've been corresponding with someone."

His heart rate picked up. This was a rude awakening. "Okay, and they've come to find you?"

"No, they've come to find *you*. It's that pediatrician I've been telling you about."

Miles groaned. "Bella."

"What? I was honest with her. I told her that I liked her, but how you weren't really interested in anything, and how disappointed I was."

He rubbed his face with his hands. "You told her I wasn't interested in her, and she still showed up?"

"It's not like that! She said she happened to be coming to the island for a weekend getaway, and I said we'd love to meet her."

Miles sat in the morning light, his face resting in his hands. Truthfully, he should only be surprised it hadn't happened sooner.

"I see," he finally said.

"You promised you wouldn't be mad!" Bella pulled a hand off his face.

"I'm not mad," he said slowly. "But *I* didn't make any promises about seeing this woman, so I don't know why I need to pick her up from the ferry."

"*Dad*," Bella bemoaned, "she's really nice and really smart. Don't you think I deserve a nice stepmom? She's a good influence, too. She's a doctor!"

As if that was the key to sending Bella off to medical school. The real issue was Miles finding a way to survive Bella's conniving years with her repeatedly outsmarting him. Or would it be decades of this?

He shuddered at the thought.

"That's if she even is who she says she is. What if the person you've been corresponding with is actually a fifty-year-old man? What if he's come looking for you?"

"Ew, Dad. Be serious."

He laughed. "I am serious. Don't they teach you about the dangers of the internet at school? Isn't there some movie I can scare you with?"

She stood taller, running her hands over her blouse. "Well, her ferry's going to be here in thirty minutes, so you need to get dressed."

How did she keep outmaneuvering him? Was there a movie *he* could watch?

Miles shut his eyes. He had promised he wouldn't be mad. If he ever wanted her to come to him with real problems, he had to stick to that.

But meeting some desperate stranger from the internet was the last thing he wanted to do with his weekend. He opened his eyes and formed a protest, but Bella was gone.

He got up, got dressed, and threw back a cup of coffee. They got to the ferry with time to spare, then stood back watching.

"Is she going to bring a red rose or something?" Miles asked.

Bella shot him a look. "She won't need to. I'll recognize her."

"Or him," Miles muttered. "It still could be a fifty-year-old man."

No response.

A blonde woman in hiking clothes stepped off the ferry, rolling a suitcase beside her. Bella waved at her wildly.

"She's not an old man. See!"

Miles frowned. "I wouldn't say fifty is old, but – "

"Over here!" Bella flailed her arms.

The woman caught sight of her, and her face brightened. Miles watched warily as she approached, remembering the pictures Bella had shown him months prior.

To be fair, she looked just like them – big eyes, short blonde hair, and a slim figure. She was, by all measures, attractive.

"Bella! It's so nice to finally meet you." She clasped Bella's hand with both of hers. She turned to Miles. "I'm sure this is very strange for you, Miles. I'm Gemma Birch."

He offered her a handshake. There was no need to be rude. "A bit of a surprise, I can admit."

She had the sort of warm smile that reached her eyes. They were blue and clear, framed with slight wrinkles. Her smile looked honest. "Well, please don't let me impose on your weekend. I – "

"Should we all get breakfast?" Bella asked brightly. "I'm really hungry, Dad. I'm starting to get dizzy, actually."

He shot her a lazy look. "I'm sure Dr. Birch has plans."

"Please, call me Gemma. And not exactly. I try to come up to the islands as much as I can to enjoy the calm and the hiking."

"The islands are good for that," he said.

His stomach growled. There was no use pretending he didn't want breakfast, and maybe if he entertained Bella's attempt at setting him up, she'd finally stop doing it.

"There's a great breakfast joint in town," he said. "I feel I owe you that much, since my daughter lured you here under false pretenses."

Bella's eyes bulged. "*Dad!*"

Gemma laughed. "There was nothing false about them. The billboard made me laugh out loud. I don't know what possessed me to send the email but...here I am."

She shrugged, a smile still broadly on her face.

Bella looked at him, her eyes full of hope.

How could he explain to her that life wasn't a Hallmark Christmas movie?

He could start by making her watch one. Or by showing her that when a real person showed up, it was far more complicated than the movies.

"Shall we?" he said.

Twenty-three

There was no reason to worry. Things were going according to plan – positively, even.

Except anything positive triggered Annie's suspicion. Things never went well for Annie, at least not recently. She'd had a slew of bad luck, and it felt like the natural flow of her life now. Her husband running off, not being able to finish her PhD, losing her home, losing her future...

Anything that went against the trend seemed fake.

Yet as she stood in the cramped bedroom she shared with her mother, staring at her sparkling reflection in the mirror, she had the tiniest hope things might be turning around.

The week prior brought the custody and child support hearing with Roy. It was done virtually and far less formally than she'd expected. Roy came prepared, flanked by a stern-looking attorney, and Annie attended by herself.

Well, sort of by herself. The judge was on her side immediately, chastising Roy for his "transparent attempt to decrease child support obligations."

"You must think," she had said, "I'm just a dumb country judge who hasn't seen this play a hundred times before."

Miles had been right about all of it. Roy's laughable attempt at full custody was called out for what it was – a ploy -- and the judge took no mercy on him.

She set a formal child support payment more than five times what Annie had asked for. She denied full custody but did implement a formal custody agreement with gradually increasing visits – one weekend a month, then two weekends a month if it went well. Roy would also be responsible for paying all costs associated with the ferry since he was the one who had chosen to move off the island.

In less than half an hour, it was over. Annie had shut her laptop and stared at the wall for a full five minutes, wading through her thoughts and riding the waves of emotions.

At first, she felt bad for Roy. She hadn't wanted it to go that way. The amount he had to pay felt shocking. Truly shocking.

It had all started because she was afraid of overdrawing her bank account every month, and after sitting with the judge's words in her head, the feeling of guilt receded.

It was plainly obvious, even to a stranger, what Roy was up to. The judge had called his behavior "borderline abandonment."

It wasn't in Annie's head. It wasn't an exaggeration. And it wasn't her fault.

After the hearing, she threw herself into the whirlwind of last minute preparations for the fundraiser. It came together beautifully, likely because of Margie. She was not just an expert at throwing events, but a darling who could get anything from anyone just by flashing a smile.

The auction for the fundraiser had everything: a sunset sailing cruise with a dinner by a private chef, rock climbing lessons, a year's supply of fresh oysters, a helicopter ride for a weekend getaway on a private estate, an oil painting of Friday Harbor, a handmade wooden canoe – it was incredible, and the support from the community was unmatched.

The guest list was packed, a local band volunteered their services in exchange for dinner, and Annie had a babysitter and this beautiful gown.

She stared at her reflection, the sequined flowers catching in the light, the fabric clinging to her curves, and her hair falling around her shoulders in loose waves.

Annie took a deep breath. For the first time in what felt like years, she felt pretty.

Could things really be turning around for her? Was there any chance that Miles would take notice of her? In this gown, with this makeup, without yogurt in her hair, might he *see* her?

He would be there in a tuxedo, apparently, as the firemen had made a point to rent them for the event. They didn't know this, but they were to be honored at the end of the night. It was Margie's idea. They'd surely be in high demand all night, but maybe Annie could ask Miles for a dance, if she were so bold.

It was easy enough to pass off as something a friend would do. As far as she knew, he wasn't bringing a date, either.

Although a few weeks prior, right around Valentine's Day, she'd seen Miles out with a woman. She was quite pretty, casually sitting and laughing with Miles and Bella over breakfast.

Annie had caught a glimpse of them as she passed by, carting the twins off to swim lessons, when she had seen them. He'd never mentioned anyone, though, and never said he had a Valentine.

In fact, he'd gotten Annie a box of chocolates, local and exquisite – not that she had any illusions that she was his Valentine.

He never talked about the woman, and neither did Bella. It could've been an aunt, or a cousin. Annie couldn't stop thinking about it, but it seemed like nothing out of the ordinary for the two of them, so...

Annie wasn't going to let herself be defeated by her own thoughts. Not today. She was going to shed her sad persona and go to this fundraiser disguised as a pretty woman. She was going to see Miles there. She was going to talk to him, and maybe even dance with him.

She slipped on a pair of heels and headed out the door.

. . .

Miles had offered to give her a ride, but Annie wanted to get there early to help Margie with any last-minute issues.

Of course, there was nothing for her to do. She pulled up to Saltwater Cove and parked her car. Margie's husband Hank was there welcoming early arrivers and vendors.

"Looking snazzy," he said with a nod.

It was rare to see him out of his sheriff uniform. Even when Annie saw him at home wearing a t-shirt, he looked authoritative. "You too, Hank."

The barn at Saltwater Cove was dressed for the occasion. Margie had a stunning flower arch filled with roses and hydrangeas at the entry – perfect for people to take pictures. Inside the barn, the band was setting up under warm lights, the tables were draped in beautiful linens and topped with more flowers.

Annie walked the grounds slowly, taking in the details. The sky was a band of bright blue. The ocean was calm, granting them a reprieve from wind. They had been blessed with unusually warm weather for the season. Despite this, Margie was prepared for the party to go late into the night, with gas-powered heaters standing every few feet outside.

"Margie, this is magnificent," Annie said when they met outside of the barn.

"No, *you* are magnificent," she stepped back, holding both of her hands.

Annie could only roll her eyes. Margie was dressed in a stunning white gown threaded with delicate lace, and flowers in her hair.

"You look lovely."

"Thank you!"

"I am so excited for today." Annie took a deep breath, pushing away the negative thoughts. "What can I do to help?"

Margie tapped her chin. "I'd like you to enjoy yourself. You've been a huge part of the magic."

Annie beamed. "Thanks, Margie."

Over the course of the next twenty minutes, the venue went from beautiful and empty to suddenly full of people and activity: swooshing dresses, booming laughter, and guests with their arms around each other's shoulders, smiling for pictures.

Annie's head was spinning. Everyone was here – vendors she'd worked with, people who had donated, people she knew from church and daycare -- yet, no Miles.

She was busy fetching bottles of water for the band, constantly scanning the crowd, when she spotted a familiar face.

At first, she thought she was seeing things. There was no way the woman at the bar could be the same woman she'd seen out with Miles.

Annie dropped off the waters before discreetly making her way back to the bar, weaving through the revelers until she got close enough to confirm.

Yes, it was her, dressed in a strapless black satin gown, her blonde hair twisted into a complicated knot at the nape of her neck.

Mile's mystery woman, even more gorgeous than Annie remembered.

Her heart sunk into her stomach. This woman had to be Miles' date. Why else would she be here, standing and laughing, bright and happy?

Heat burned on Annie's skin. She stumbled her way to the bathroom and locked the door behind her, dabbing water on the back of her neck. She almost splashed water on her face, remembering at the last second she was wearing makeup.

Of course Miles had a date. Why wouldn't he? He was the fire department's most eligible bachelor.

And who was Annie? A friend. A neighbor. A charity case on occasion, but nothing more.

It took her several minutes to regain her composure, and when she emerged from the bathroom, someone called her name.

She thought she might have to face him, but it was only Lauren.

Annie stopped dead in her tracks. "What are you doing here?"

Lauren screwed up her face, opening her mouth in mock surprise. "That's how I'm greeted!"

"You don't even like the firefighters," Annie said. She was too emotionally fried to find kinder words.

Lauren cast a look over her shoulder. "What? I never said that."

"You don't seem to have a problem with the company ripping them off for fire truck parts, and now you're here at the fundraiser?"

Lauren grabbed her arm and pulled her aside. "What is going on with you, Annie?"

She caught sight of the beautiful woman again. Recklessness surged in her chest. "Where did you get that Porsche, Lauren?"

"Annie," she whispered. "Keep your voice down. It's not what you think."

"I don't know what to think."

"You don't understand," she said, her eyes round. "We needed that car."

Annie stared at her as understanding threatened to break through the emotional storm in her head. "What?"

She hadn't been accusing her of anything, but Lauren was ready with a confession.

"I'm not against the firefighters. I'm against weak cases."

"Weak cases," Annie repeated slowly.

A shout rang out, and both Annie and Lauren looked to the crowd.

Lauren let out a groan. "Oh, no. It's Alex."

"Who is that?" Annie asked.

"My brother," she said with a sigh.

Annie didn't even know Lauren had a brother. Apparently, there was a lot she didn't know about her friend.

"He was in a relationship with Clarissa, one of the firefighters. They ended things a few months ago, and he hasn't taken it well. I mean, *he's* not well. I'm surprised he showed up here."

By the looks of it, no one else seemed terribly shocked. Hank already had the unruly sweatpant-clad man by the arm, spinning him around and walking him out like a perp.

Miles appeared at Hank's side, his broad shoulders filling out a sleek black tuxedo. He stood tall and handsome, like something out of a dream.

Annie watched, mesmerized, as he spoke to Hank and Alex. When Hank disappeared, Miles turned. He caught her eye, a broad smile crossing his face.

Her heart, the traitor, fluttered against her ribcage.

Twenty-four

He could still hear Alex yelling as Hank dragged him away.

"You ripped us apart for nothing, Miles!"

The words barely registered. He wasn't the first firefighter Alex had accused of seducing Clarissa, and he wouldn't be the last. A few months prior, Alex had broken into the fire station, climbing through a window after seeing Clarissa eating chili with Miles and Sam.

They had all been stunned to see him, cut off mid-laugh a discussion about a call for a water rescue that ended up being a large coat that had blown into the ocean.

Any thought of the jealous man disappeared from Miles' mind the moment he saw Annie. He'd been looking for her since arriving at the fundraiser – late, due to a disaster with Bella's hair.

She'd gone into town to get it done with a friend, bringing along pictures of a complicated updo. An hour later, she came home sobbing and said she would not attend the fundraiser.

"What if Noah sees me like this?" she had wailed.

Miles had shrugged, narrowing his eyes on the curls and pins in her dark hair. "Honestly, he probably isn't going to notice."

That wasn't the comfort he thought it would be. Bella had cried out and thrown herself onto the couch.

He had been at a loss. The only thing he could think of was a story Annie had told him about her mom doing her hair for all the school dances when she was growing up. It took a lot of coaxing, but he convinced her to go down the street and show Clara the damage.

An hour and a lot of tears later, Clara was able to carefully disassemble the hairdo and put in its place an intricate and swooping braid. Bella cried again – tears of joy this time – and they rushed home so she could finish getting ready.

They were nearly two hours late to the fundraiser. He thought about texting Annie to let her know, but it seemed presumptuous. Why would Annie be waiting on him?

Then, all of a sudden, she appeared like an apparition of his mind, dressed in shimmering gold and catching the light like a diamond. Her dress was stunning, covered in flowers blooming over her curves and daring his gaze to drift down the deep neckline.

His heart hammered in his chest and the room emptied around him. All he could see was her. There was a perfect clearing between them, as though he were looking at her preparing to walk down the aisle.

The thought of it forced a lump into his throat.

A smile graced her beautiful face, her eyes lighting up at the sight of him. And since he wasn't a groom standing and waiting for his bride, he could go to her, which he did – happily.

"Annie," he said when he reached her, the intoxicating scent of her rose perfume throwing him momentarily. "I've been looking for you."

"Ah, you didn't recognize me." She shook her head, looking down at herself. "I know. I feel like an imposter."

Miles scowled. "You're not an imposter. You look stunning." He wanted to add that she always looked stunning, but instead, he held his breath, waiting to see if his words had any effect on her.

But she just laughed her easy laugh. "You're looking very dapper in your station-issued tuxedo."

He tipped his head. "Thank you. I feel a bit like James Bond, especially after helping to kick Alex out." He cleared his throat. "That's my co-worker Cassandra's ex-boyfriend. He's made a nuisance of himself."

"Sorry about him," a woman's voice said.

He raised his eyebrows. The woman next to Annie was speaking. He hadn't noticed her until now.

"This is Lauren," Annie said, noticing his surprise. "Our kids go to daycare together."

"Unfortunately, Alex is my brother." Lauren stuck out her hand, a bright smile on her face. "It's so nice to meet you. I've heard so much about you."

He cast a glance at Annie, but she said nothing. Had she really been talking about him? Or had it been Alex?

"I'm sorry about my brother. He's never been quite the same since falling off that cliffside." She let out a loud laugh.

Miles looked at Annie, narrowing his eyes, and she lifted a dainty shoulder in a shrug, as if to say, "I don't know if she's kidding."

"Maybe Roy needs to take a tumble off of a mountainside," Miles said, chancing a smile. "Might knock some sense into him."

Annie covered her mouth with her hand, laughing. "Is that a threat?"

"Not unless you want it to be." He paused, pretending to think. "Though I don't think I need to threaten him now. The judge did a good job of that."

Lauren turned to her. "You never told me about that!"

Interesting. Miles knew more about Annie's life than this friend. Was it possible that Annie trusted him more? Liked him more?

"I've been busy," Annie said, shaking her head. "It went pretty well."

"I'm so glad to hear it."

Miles wasn't going to cede the floor to the lesser friend. He caught Annie's gaze. "I'm sorry I was late. Bella had a hair emergency."

Annie groaned. "Oh no! What happened?"

He shrugged. "A bad updo, I guess. Your mom went through several different braids before finding one that Bella would accept."

"Poor Bella." Annie scanned the crowd. "I don't see her, but I'm glad my mom could help. She's always been a wizard with hair."

"Yeah, I remember you saying that."

He couldn't stop staring at her. She was mesmerizing.

Her gaze fell back on him, catching his stare.

Miles cleared his throat. "This is really phenomenal, Annie. I'm so thankful to you and Margie. Let's be honest—I'm especially thankful to you, for thinking of this and putting it together."

Her chest rose and fell with a deep breath. "Well, thank you for saving us from fires."

He rolled his eyes. "Lately we've been responding to low blood sugars, drunk drivers, and cats stuck in trees that end up being raccoons."

She flashed a smile but said nothing.

Normally he could read her face, find the slightest hint of stress or worry or joy.

Now, though, it was as if she was blocked in some way. Was she overwhelmed? Excited? Was her friend not really a friend?

Something wasn't right. He needed to find out what it was. He needed to create an excuse to spend the rest of the evening with her. Staring at her now, it became clear to him that it was imperative to keep her on his arm, not just tonight, but every night.

Someone grabbed his arm from behind. Miles turned to see Gemma, of all people.

"Oh, hey, Dr. Birch," he said, keeping his tone light. The surprise of seeing her blew over him like a wind.

He turned to introduce Gemma to Annie, but Annie was already slipping into the crowd.

He wanted to go after her, but he couldn't be so rude to Gemma. He turned to her. "I must admit, I did not expect to see you here. Is this another one of Bella's setups?"

Gemma laughed, throwing her head back. "I swear it isn't, and I'm not stalking you. A friend of mine asked me to come to this. He was a doctor in our practice, but he retired to the island a few years ago."

"Aha, so you're trying to follow in his footsteps," Miles said.

She let out a breath. "Yeah, I've only got about twenty years left to retirement."

He leaned back on his heels. "I'm sure they could use a pediatrician on the island if you'd like to move sooner."

She stared at him for a long moment. Long enough for Miles to realize what he'd just said.

"I wonder that myself," Gemma said graciously.

Though they'd had a pleasant breakfast together, Miles had no interest in dating this woman. Bella hadn't been bringing it up as frequently, likely because she was involved with Noah, who was also wandering around somewhere.

It was best to clear the air. "Listen, I'm sorry about Bella pulling you into all this, but – "

Gemma put up a hand. "Please. We don't have to do that. I really was just curious about the man on the billboard."

He smiled, shaking his head. "Aren't we all? He seems great."

"It was such a wild romantic comedy sort of idea. Sometimes those things work out, you know? You have to take risks."

Risks. The idea of it sent goosebumps over his arms. That was one thing he didn't like, even as a firefighter. Especially so.

"Of course," he said with a nod.

Margie appeared at his side, pulling him in for a hug. Naturally, she already knew Gemma. It made it easy for him to slip away in search of Annie.

Except Clarissa cornered him.

"I debated telling you this," she said.

His eyes strained over the crowd. Where could Annie have gone?

He cleared his throat. "Debated telling me what?"

Clarissa lowered her voice. "It's embarrassing. It's about Alex."

"You shouldn't be embarrassed about Alex. It's not your fault he is the way he is."

She sighed. "Yeah, well, for some reason he's fixated on you now. I guess the billboards drove him extra crazy."

His mouth tilted in a half smile. "I have the tendency to do that."

"Gross." She punched him in the arm. "*Listen* to me."

He stopped looking around and focused his attention on her. "What's up?"

"I had an anonymous letter dropped off at my door."

"Is that a signature Alex move?"

"I guess," she shrugged. "It said my new boyfriend would get to watch his world burn around him. I can only assume he means you, even though I find you disgusting and would never date you."

Miles knew she wasn't just saying that; she fully meant it, always treating him like an annoying little brother. "You're too sweet."

"I'm serious. I wish he wasn't fixated on you, but he is. He can be dangerous. I'm so sorry you're getting dragged into this."

If Alex was targeting him, what's the worst he could do? Surely he wouldn't be dumb enough to actually come after Miles?

Or would he come after someone else? Someone like...Bella?

A zing reverberated through his nerves, from his hands down to his feet. If Alex did anything to Bella, if he as much looked at her the wrong way, he was done.

Blood pumped into his ears and he forced himself to take a breath. "I know how he can be. I will tell Bella to look out for him, and if he comes anywhere near me – well, he won't be able to write letters anymore."

Clarissa stared at him for a long beat. Then, she took a deep breath and said, "Okay."

After breaking free from *that* conversation, another group pulled him in – some of the volunteer firefighters. He talked to them, leaving as soon as it was polite, and kept looking for

Annie. Every time he tried to break away from whatever group had sucked him in, he stumbled into another conversation.

It reminded him of when he was a groom at his wedding. He barely got a chance to eat or drink anything before the night was over, then he and Madeline had collapsed into bed that night exhausted and delirious.

What would Madeline make of this night? What would she have thought of Bella's hair disaster, her date with Noah?

Of Annie?

It was bizarre to think of it, but he was sure they would've gotten along under different circumstances.

He finally found Annie again. She was talking to a large group. He tried to elbow in next to her, but as soon as he arrived, she excused herself and disappeared into the crowd.

By the end of the night, he'd seemingly talked to everyone at the fundraiser except Annie. It was hard to shake the feeling she was avoiding him.

Perhaps he'd finally gone too far, making a nuisance of himself. She clearly had another life, a full life, that didn't involve him showing up at her door all the time.

As the night went on, it became impossible for him to ignore. Annie was not waiting around for Miles. She was not looking for him and didn't want to spend the evening alongside him.

By chasing her, he was no better than Alex, in some ways. If she'd wanted to talk to him, she would have. If she'd wanted to dance with him, she easily could have.

He stopped chasing her. Miles told himself it was better this way. As he was about to tell Gemma, he didn't have the space in his life for anyone else. There was only space for Bella – and apparently, Bella's hair. He had no interest in dating, no interest in finding a girlfriend or a wife or anything. That was as true today as it was when Bella put up that cursed billboard.

At the end of the evening, Margie surprised all of them with an award she'd made up: "Best Firefighters on San Juan Island."

As goofy as it was, it was fun to accept it and stand for pictures. As he stood in the crowd, looking out into the flashes, he caught a glimpse of Annie. She was leaning against the bar, her eyes on him for the briefest of moments, before disappearing again.

All in all, it was a magnificent evening. They'd raised nearly two hundred thousand dollars, everyone had a great time, and he had gotten to catch up with people he didn't always get to see.

Yet when he went home unsettled that night, something kept nagging at him. No matter how many times he pushed it away, it kept popping back into his mind.

If it were so true that he could so easily turn down all these women, and he had no interest in them, why, *why* could he not fall asleep without thinking one last time of Annie?

Twenty-five

For months she had wondered – dared to hope, really – that Miles felt something for her. That there was something more to his lingering looks and his thoughtful words.

At least now she knew the truth.

It was absurd. *She* was absurd. To think that a most eligible bachelor would turn his nose up at hundreds of women only to fall in love with *her*?

She'd truly lost it this time.

Vanity had never been one of her flaws, but she now realized she must have a blind spot. Despite knowing – and believing – she was unappealing to the opposite sex, somehow she still thought Miles might have seen something in her. Something that Annie hadn't even seen.

Maybe there were good things about her, but that had all been before. Before getting married. Before a challenging twin pregnancy. Before Roy left.

Annie was a woman who had been left. As much as she tried not to think about it, and while it was far more important to think about the effect on the twins, there was an effect on her, too.

She was someone who *could* be left. She wasn't someone worth staying with, in Roy's eyes, and he'd known her so well. The best of anyone, perhaps.

What did that say about her? When her world was on fire, when she was drowning, she wasn't worth saving.

Tears flooded her eyes.

She brushed them away and focused on her computer screen. It was a quiet day at the lab outpost. She was the only one there; she could get a lot of work done. She *needed* to get a lot of work done, not waste her time running over every detail of the fundraiser again and again – looping Miles in her mind, impossibly handsome in his tuxedo, standing tall and laughing with that beautiful doctor.

Of course he'd found a gorgeous doctor to be his date. Why shouldn't he? She had the kindest eyes. She looked genuinely nice. He deserved someone like that, and she was truly happy for him. She only wished she hadn't been so foolish.

The longer she chewed through her thoughts, the gentler she could be with herself. It wasn't her fault she'd developed a crush on him. She was only human. Maybe it had been a coping mechanism to get through a difficult time.

And hadn't she gotten through? Weren't things better now? She'd come a long way. Most days, she didn't feel like a total failure and she wasn't drowning. Not really.

Her mom was getting better, and now, thanks to Roy's court mandated generosity, she could afford everything the twins needed and more.

Roy was even making an effort to see the kids more often. Apparently, the judge's reprimand had an effect on him. To Annie, it was like a peek at Old Roy, the one she'd known so well. Old Roy would have been horrified to be scolded by an authority figure.

Then again, Old Roy had talked about how he couldn't wait to play catch with his kids in the backyard. Old Roy dreamt of baking Christmas cookies and reading bedtime stories.

Perhaps Old Roy had been too naïve. He'd failed to imagine the chronic exhaustion, the back-to-back illness, the absorption of his free time and the tears – the kids' and his own.

He'd only imagined the fun parts. The picture-perfect moments.

Maybe he'd still have those one day. Annie truly hoped he'd redeem himself, for the twins' sake. Then, if Annie could pull herself together enough, Leon and Noel would have an okay set of parents.

Enough. That was the word. She just needed to be *enough*. Not perfect, but a good *enough* mother.

It was constantly on her mind. Did she love them enough? Did she show them how much she loved them enough? Did she fight for them enough?

She certainly worried about them enough.

For the first time in a year, she felt the answer to these questions might be a yes, or at least, a maybe. She was getting there.

Miles had played no small role in that. In the end, wasn't friendship more important than romance? At least as a friend, he was less likely to leave her.

Annie rubbed her face with her hands and stood. She needed to grab a stack of research papers she'd left upstairs.

She ran up to the third floor, the door to the staircase slamming behind her. This was not the most organized part of the lab. They'd all wanted to tidy it up, but who had the time? It was a place to store forgotten projects and old papers.

She weaved through the stacks of storage boxes until she found one she'd labeled and abandoned six months before. It was only supposed to be a few weeks, but oops. Life happened.

Annie settled into a chair and slowly lifted out the folders inside, searching for the one paper she had a vague memory of.

This was good. Her chest didn't feel quite as heavy. She could accept the reality of Miles having a girlfriend without having to lie to herself. It'd be a blatant lie to herself, and to the universe, to say she didn't want more, but the friendship was still good, even if, right now, it filled her with deep sadness. Like she told the twins all the time, "It's okay to feel sad," and "It's okay to feel angry." Though she always had to add, "It's not okay to hit."

She laughed out loud to herself, sucking in a sharp breath like the madwoman she was.

The air burned and a cough erupted from her chest. Annie cleared her throat. It smelled like a campfire. Who would be irresponsible enough to have a campfire at this time of year?

She stood and peered out of the window. Her heart jumped. A car was parked next to hers. For a second, she thought it was Miles coming to visit her, but it wasn't his truck. It was a blue sedan, the paint on the hood peeling, garbage piled in the passenger seat.

Definitely not Miles' car. A dark figure sat in the driver's seat. Annie gazed down, and a pair of eyes looked up at her.

Annie squinted. She couldn't make out the person's face. She thought about waving, but it seemed too absurd. Could they even see her?

Whoever it was scrambled and flailed as they started the car, which abruptly flew backwards.

The hairs on the back of Annie's neck stood up. Something wasn't right with that. She had never felt unsafe being at the outpost alone, but something here was off. Maybe she'd call her boss and see if he'd sent someone out.

Except she'd left her phone downstairs at her desk. Annie turned and jogged to the staircase door, her heart thundering in her chest. A cough caught in her throat the same moment the smoke detector released a shrill cry.

Annie pulled the door open. The staircase was engulfed in flames. A scream rang out. Only after she'd slammed the door did she realize it was her own voice.

She was entirely alone.

Twenty-six

The minutes refused to pass by. Miles sat in the fire station's kitchen, his legs up on a chair, his hands behind his head, staring at the clock.

Tick. Tick. Tick.

There wasn't much excitement this shift. A call had gone out an hour prior for a small brush fire, and Sam had taken the working truck and met up with a few of the volunteer firefighters. He thought it would be a good teaching experience.

Miles and Clarissa stayed behind. The mood was odd. Clarissa seemed to be avoiding him, hiding behind a large paperback book.

He assumed she felt sheepish about the Alex situation, but as he'd told her, none of it was her fault. Miles had a talk with Bella about it, and in true teenage hubris, her main response was, "Ew, weird!"

Chief Hank was aware of the situation as well, and the second that Alex stepped out of line, he'd be hauled off to jail and hit with the harshest charges they could muster.

It seemed tidy enough for the time being, but it left him with a lingering, uneasy feeling every time it crossed his mind. Luckily, his mind was preoccupied with someone else.

He let out a long sigh. Annie had been so stunning that night, so elegant and enchanting. All he'd wanted the entire time was to be near to her, to steal a glance of her in that glittering gown.

Yet, for whatever reason, he couldn't find her, and he could no longer deny that she must not have wanted to be found. It was all fine and dandy when he showed up on her doorstep, but she wasn't looking for him. She wasn't longing for him the way he longed for her.

Looking back, it had always been him making the moves. He was the one who had invited her to Thanksgiving and then pulled her into that ridiculous dance. He was the one who took her stargazing and nearly smothered her with a kiss.

Annie was upfront about her life and her situation. She was recovering from a painful divorce. She wasn't one of those women who sent a resume and a headshot to Bella's email. She had never even asked him to come over. He was supposed to install a handrail and get out of her life.

He just couldn't find the way to do that.

The fire bell went off. Miles jumped from his seat, and Clarissa from hers. They ran off and dressed: pants, boots, hoods, coats, air tanks, helmets, gloves, radios. Miles moved steadily with practiced hands, his mind centered by one of the few things that could rip his focus from Annie.

Clarissa got to the firetruck first and the call came over with the address: "Fire reported at the microbiology lab outpost, west side of the island. Call reporting heavy smoke and flames visible. Time out 14:25."

He froze, ice running through his veins. That was where Annie worked.

"Start the truck now!" he bellowed.

"It won't start," Clarissa yelled back.

His chest felt so tight that it was hard to take a breath. "There isn't time for this. I'll meet you there."

Miles grabbed a ladder and a box of supplies, sprinting to his truck, every fiber in his body on fire, working in unison.

His pickup truck ripped out of the parking lot, Miles at the helm. His hands gripped the steering wheel, his breath heaving in his chest. The only sound was the wind gasping into the open windows.

He got on the radio. They'd put out a call for Sam to bring the other fire truck. Good. He'd still beat them there.

Three minutes away. He was making good time, but it was still taking too long. If only his truck had a siren...

He activated his phone with his voice and called Annie – no answer.

He called her mom. She picked up promptly.

"Hello?"

"Clara, it's Miles." He kept his voice steady, refusing to allow any panic in. "Is Annie at the lab today?"

"Yes, she is. Why?"

He swallowed. He'd known. The moment that fire bell went off, he'd felt it somewhere deep inside of him, in some chamber of his heart that was forever connected to hers.

It was best to keep Clara calm. "Sorry, I'm in a hurry," he said. "I need to drop something off for her."

"Okay, tell her I love her!"

His chest tightened, a crack forming in his stoic resolve. "I will."

He saw the smoke before he got there – a black column rising to the sky. The building loomed against the absurd backdrop of the sparkling sea, three stories of wood and brick, a sheet of orange flame licking the roof.

His stomach lurched.

Annie's car was alone in the parking lot.

"Dispatch, be advised this is a three-story commercial structure, heavy fire involvement, ground to roof. Call a third alarm."

Not waiting for a response, he skidded his truck to a halt and leapt out. He pulled up his hood, pressed his mask against his face, tightened the straps and inhaled sharply before opening the gas canister.

Air flowed. He activated the PASS device on his helmet and it chirped at him. Good to go.

He was not waiting on anyone else to show up. If he stopped moving, they'd hear the device screaming for help.

He kicked the door open and disappeared inside.

Twenty-seven

Annie should have jumped out of the window when she had the chance. Now, it was too late. She was stuck. Trapped.

Her voice was hoarse from screaming for help – or maybe it was the smoke. She wasn't sure. She'd stayed at the window yelling as long as she could, but the fire moved so quickly and the smoke was so overpowering. She had no choice but to flee into a small office at the back corner of the building where she could shut the door.

A small, windowless room. She sat on the floor, trying to catch the last breaths of smokeless air. Did anyone even know the building was on fire? The person in the parking lot might have, though as soon as they had seen her looking out the window, they had scurried off.

There was nothing else nearby, just some houses on the other side of the wall of trees. Would anyone notice the smoke? There had to be at least one busybody at home, someone curious enough to find out what was going on.

If only she hadn't committed so fully to detaching from her phone. Months ago, she'd realized she had the bad habit of staring at it too much. It was a way to soothe her anxiety around the divorce, mindlessly scrolling through pictures and videos. The bad habit had bled into her work life and into her home life, so she had put a stop to it.

Annie hadn't even thought twice about leaving her phone behind, sitting at her desk. And now she had no way to call for help.

Maybe she could still jump out of the window? She crawled to the door on her knees and cracked it open. Black smoke poured in, and she shut the door in a fit of coughing.

Even if she could find the window, what if she couldn't hold her breath long enough to get to it? When she'd looked down before, it was dizzying. It seemed so high. Could she survive a fall from that height? She'd certainly break her legs, but what was two broken legs if she still had her life?

Tears rushed into her eyes. She should've stayed downstairs. She shouldn't have come to work at all. She should have set up a will – not that she had anything to leave to the kids, but maybe she could've written them letters. A final goodbye, so they could know she had loved them so, so dearly.

The tears spilled out with a sob. Annie put her face in her hands and let it out.

"Annie!"

She stopped, her chest rising and falling rapidly as she tried to stop crying.

It was so faint she thought she was imagining it.

"Annie!"

She sat up. There it was again. A muffled voice, but it was there.

She stood from her crouched position and screamed, "Help! I'm in here!"

The smoke was so thick and dark she couldn't see the door anymore, until a moment later when it burst open and a beam of light pierced the darkness.

"Annie."

She still couldn't see who was calling her name, but she could hear him now. She ran towards the light and slammed into a mass of yellow.

He wore a mask, and the light blinded her, but even through the smoke and chaos, she knew who it was.

Miles.

A sob caught in her throat, and coughing overtook her again. She collapsed into his arms, and with one motion, he swept her up, moving powerful legs swiftly through the hazy darkness.

A window burst open, the crisp outside air quickly polluted by smoke.

"Ladder!" he yelled, and within seconds, metal slammed against the building.

"Can you make it out?"

She nodded, coughing.

Miles leapt out first, and Annie second. He guided her down as she continued coughing and wheezing.

On the ground, he picked her up again, running to a waiting ambulance.

He set her down. "Is there anyone else inside?" he asked, staring at her through the mask.

She had the nonsensical thought that his eyes looked so pretty in this light.

Annie managed to shake her head, and the medics swarmed her, wrapping her in blankets, pressing oxygen to her face, asking her questions.

Miles stood behind them and removed his mask, his expression hard. He waited only a moment before disappearing.

There were two fire trucks there, hoses going, people yelling, and all at once the realization hit her – she wasn't going to die.

Not today, at least.

Annie tilted her head back and looked at the sky, finally able to take a full breath.

. . .

After a trip to the hospital to be checked out and treated for smoke inhalation, Annie was sent home.

The days that followed were a blur of calls and visits and a seemingly endless parade of flowers.

It was too much to process. The building, despite the best efforts of the fire department, was lost. All their data for the lab was gone.

When the head of the lab came to see her, Annie openly mourned the loss of their research.

He stared at her for a moment, a look of bewilderment on his face. "Annie," he leaned in, eyebrows furrowed, "it's a shame, of course, but all I care about is that you're alive."

This made her burst into guilt-filled tears.

There were a lot of tears over the coming days, most of them between her and her mom. Annie caught her mom staring at her more than once before bursting into tears.

"Mom," she'd groan. "I'm fine!"

Her mom would only sniffle, hug her, and fuss away.

Annie most certainly was not fine, but she wasn't going to burden anyone with it. Mercifully, the twins had no idea anything had happened. All they knew was Mom was home a lot more the following week, which meant more time to fight for her attention.

The normalcy of their reaction was comforting, because horrifyingly, even Roy called, panic evident in his voice.

"Are you sure you're okay?" he asked.

"I'm fine," she lied, because if there was anyone she was going to talk to about how she felt, it wasn't Roy.

Two days after the smolders were out, she met with Chief Hank and a special fire investigator. She told them what she'd seen from the window when the fire started. They cast each other a look but said nothing.

Annie was desperate to know what had happened. She asked Hank if he knew about the threat against the fire department. He only nodded.

She wanted to tell him about Lauren – the cavalier way she'd talked about the fire department losing their case. The way she'd gotten an extremely expensive car out of the blue, how it seemed she'd almost confessed something at the fundraiser.

It all seemed connected, but the thought was too horrible to entertain. How could Annie tell Hank about it if she didn't even know what was going on? She wasn't going to accuse Lauren of starting the fire. It was too insane. Saying her friend had tried to kill her? Over *what?*

Annie's head spun even thinking of it. Perhaps she was a terrible judge of character after all.

She decided to hold her tongue until she was sure whatever she reported was the truth. Chief Hank seemed to know what he was doing, and to top it off, the entire community was up in arms. A reward was raised for information, and another team was brought in to examine the wreckage.

Everyone was talking about it.

Everyone except Miles.

Since his heroic rescue, he'd made himself scarce. The night of the fire, he stopped by the house and stood in the doorway,

"You're feeling okay? The doctors checked you out?"

Annie nodded, still unable to put the experience into words. "I don't know how to thank you for what you did."

"I was just doing my job," he said gruffly.

His expression was hard, and there was no laughter in his eyes.

"You saved my life," she whispered. "You risked your life to save mine."

"All part of the job." He looked down, shaking his head. "Let me know if you need anything."

And with that, he turned his big, broad shoulders and walked away.

A week later and still not a word. Not a check in, not a stop by. Only Bella came to visit, and despite inviting Miles along, he never appeared.

Where had the warmth gone in their friendship? It could be as simple as him moving on. He had a new girlfriend, and maybe he realized their friendship could make her feel insecure.

Or maybe he'd tired of Annie – whining about Roy, struggling with one new daycare illness or the next. Almost dying in a fire.

Such a drama queen.

She'd avoided him at the fundraiser, but that was only because she couldn't bear to see him with another woman. It felt like daggers pressing into her heart.

Annie had hidden out on the beach, or when he almost spotted her, she ran into Margie's house. Anything but having to face Miles with *her* again.

Maybe that had offended him. Maybe he'd seen her for the immature woman she was. He'd still saved her life, but only because it was his job, like he said.

Duty. That's all Annie had ever been. Someone who needed help, and now that she'd had it – more than she deserved – he'd moved on.

Why couldn't she move on, too? Why couldn't it be simple? To find a way to be grateful for the things he'd done, the things he'd shown her. The things he'd awoken in her.

And for literally pulling her out of a burning building. Saving her life. Couldn't she find a way to be grateful for that?

Twenty-eight

Two weeks into the investigation, the local news reported the lab fire was suspected arson, and the island's already-frenzied obsession with the fire exploded.

Though he tried, Miles couldn't get away from it. A bystander had recorded a video of the fire and caught Miles running to the ambulance with Annie in his arms. Thankfully, her face was obscured, but his wasn't.

It initially ran with the headline: "Hero Firefighter Arrives at Structure Fire without Firetruck."

Talk about drama. He was getting recognized everywhere, even worse than with the ferry ads. People stopped him in the grocery store to thank him for being a hero, and his first thought was to ditch his cart and run.

Once the internet algorithm picked it up, the video got millions of views, and he got requests for interviews from across the country.

He declined them all.

Miles sat at the kitchen table, his laptop open, reading the newest slew of articles. The fire chief had no qualms about utilizing the press. In this most recent article, he went into detail about the fire truck failing to start, bemoaning that they still couldn't get the parts to fix it.

The report went on to describe the failed antitrust lawsuit and the local judge who had dismissed it. There were calls for the judge to be investigated, and several legal experts stated there was ample evidence to at least hear a case.

At least that was interesting. He scrolled on, a full glass of water sitting next to his hand, a well-intentioned idea he had completely forgotten now that he was as engrossed in this fire investigation as everyone else.

Then, the video of him running appeared again, plopped into the middle of the article under "related."

It landed like a slap. He couldn't read anything about the fire without running into that video.

He hardly remembered that moment. He had been working on instinct. Panic, really, that something would happen to Annie. When he had found her, she had felt so small in his arms, and she couldn't stop coughing, and he didn't know if she would breathe again or if she was hurt.

Why had they added it to this article? Because people loved a feel-good story?

There was nothing feel-good about it. Their fire engine would probably never work again, and they still needed to raise more money to get another one. Even still, it would be years before a new truck was built. They had no idea if the state case would be successful, and as far as he knew, there were no suspects in the arson case.

Nothing to feel good about at all.

He slammed his laptop shut and stood up.

"Slow down there," Bella said.

Miles jumped. "Oh, hey. I didn't know you were home."

"I snuck in, I guess." She narrowed her eyes. "Were you watching the video of your rescue again?"

"No. I hate that video."

He let out a breath, trying to dispel the tension in his voice. He pulled open the fridge door and grabbed the first thing he saw – a can of soda. He cracked it open.

Bella stood silent, watching him.

"What's up?" he asked, more defensively than he'd intended.

"How is Annie doing?" asked Bella. "Have you checked in on her?"

Miles took a long swig of soda and shook his head. "Not since the night of the fire."

"You haven't talked to her in two weeks?" Bella shook her head. "What is wrong with you?"

He made a face. "Nothing is wrong with me. By all accounts, she's doing fine."

"Did you guys have a fight or something?"

"No, Bella, we did not have a fight. I'm giving her some space. She had a big shock."

She crossed her arms over her chest. "*Men.*"

He laughed at her unconvincing attempt to lighten his mood. "What's that supposed to mean? Can't a guy save a girl from a fire anymore?"

Bella lowered her eyes, cutting him with a glare.

A jolt ran through Miles' chest. He didn't like that look. He didn't know what was coming, but it wouldn't be good.

"So you can run into a burning building, but you can't tell a woman how you feel?"

There it was.

He sighed. "That's not what this is, Bella."

She let out a dramatic groan. "Come on, Dad! I'm not blind. I know you like her."

"First you thought I was too old for her, but now I like her? I think – "

"That doesn't matter," she said, waving a hand. A smile danced on her face. "It took me a while to see it. It's actually my fault for getting too obsessed with the women responding to the ad."

"Ah yes. Dr. Birch," Miles said.

Bella nodded. "Yes. I really liked her. I still like her, for the record."

"And you don't like Annie?" Miles asked, a bit too quickly.

"Are you kidding me?" Her mouth dropped open. "I *love* Annie. I would totally take her as my stepmom."

He wasn't going to have this discussion. "Bella, you can't talk about people like that."

She rolled her eyes. "Come on, Dad. What are you afraid of?"

Everything. He was afraid of everything. He had already watched the woman he loved die in front of his eyes. He had already gone through a grief so deep and so bleak he thought he would never emerge.

But he'd had no choice. He'd had to emerge – for Bella.

He couldn't do it again. There was no question in his mind that it was not worth the risk to even consider loving someone again like that. And if there was anyone he could love again, it was Annie.

He opened his mouth to respond, stuttering out a rote, "It's not that simple."

"Why not?" she demanded.

"Because we're not teenagers going to the school dance, Bella."

"She's perfect, Dad!" Bella narrowed her eyes. "This is the only thing I want. I never get *anything* I want!"

He almost turned into his mother for a second, the words "Join the club" on the tip of his tongue.

That wasn't what he wanted to say, despite—for the thousandth time—feeling immense empathy for his mom all those decades ago.

He didn't know what he wanted to say. He wanted her to stop asking about it. To stop pushing. He'd worried she would hit the roof if she caught a whiff of his feelings for Annie, but he'd never expected she'd demand he marry the woman.

What crime had Annie committed to be subjected to this circus? She laughed at his jokes. She charmed. She tested his resolve, his self-control, tests that he failed time and time again.

She'd made him fall in love with her, then she almost burned up in a fire.

It was far, far too dangerous to keep seeing her, to even humor Bella's demands of wanting a stepmother.

"Yeah, well," he finally said, "you can't always get what you want."

Her face reddened, her lips forming into a pinch.

For a moment, Miles was afraid she might literally explode.

Instead, she screamed before brushing past him and disappearing out the front door.

Miles shut his eyes. He wasn't particularly proud of what he'd come up with, but there it was.

At least Bella hadn't overreacted.

Twenty-nine

It took three weeks for the smoke to clear from Annie's mind. Three weeks of lying awake in bed, staring at the wall. Three weeks of opening windows and fanning and replaying the moments of terror, stomping out the embers in her mind.

But all at once the clouds parted, and she pulled clean, crisp air into her lungs. She stared at the blackened night sky, littered with millions of burning stars. Each one was a miracle, and she was overwhelmed with gratitude and wonder.

There was a touch of terror staring back at her, too. Life was terrifying. Nearly dying was terrifying, but on the other side of that, it was an improbable miracle that any of them were here. That any of them made it on any given day.

It was the most wonderful miracle, and she wasn't going to sit idly by, questioning herself, questioning her children, waiting on Roy or anyone ever again.

Annie was going to get answers.

Chief Hank, for all his charms, was a steel trap. He wasn't giving her any hints about the investigation.

To be fair, there was a lot she wasn't telling him either, but only because she wasn't sure of the truth. With her new clarity, Annie was determined to put her fears to rest.

On Saturday morning, she asked her mom to watch the kids and texted Lauren asking for a favor.

Lauren responded quickly. "Sure, anything!"

Annie picked up coffee for them both, then pulled into Lauren's driveway. She surveyed the house for a second. There wasn't anything out of the ordinary, except for the ostentatious Porsche sitting in the sun.

She walked up to the house and just as she reached the front door, it flung open, a mass of a man flying past her, the hood of his sweatshirt over his head.

Annie stood stunned for a second, watching him gallop down the street. She cocked her head to the side. "Alex?"

Annie turned back to the house. Lauren stood in the open doorway. "Did he say where he was going?"

Annie shook her head. "Nope. I assume he's going for a midday run." She paused. "In jeans and a hoodie."

Lauren leaned out, straining her eyes down the road, her brow furrowed. "Who knows? Anyway, sorry about him. Come on in."

Annie handed Lauren her favorite – a mocha latte – then said hello to the kids. Lauren's parents were there, her mom washing dishes, her dad doing a craft. It was easy for the two of them to slip into the backyard for some privacy.

They sat in overstuffed chairs on the stone patio. Lauren's yard was expansive, spanning six acres. There was a beautiful swing set, a playhouse, and a small dirt track where the older kids rode their bikes.

"Is everything okay? You look so serious," Lauren said.

Annie sat back. She felt serious. "I'm going to ask you a favor, Lauren."

"Yeah, I know. You're making me nervous. What is it?"

Annie kept her eyes fixed on her friend. "Tell me how you got the Porsche."

Immediately, Lauren's eyes fell. "Annie, I can't."

"I need to know who gave it to you and if they had anything to do with the fire."

Lauren gasped. "Of course not! Why would you think that?" She paused. "At least...I don't think so. I mean, I would never be involved with that!"

Annie sat, her eyes fixed, her voice silent.

"I can't talk to you about this," Lauren said, lowering her voice. "The judge is already getting questions, and everyone at work is nervous."

Annie raised her coffee to her lips and took a sip.

Lauren went on. "I don't even know who gave it to me, technically. But I swear, I had nothing to do with the fire. I would *never* do anything like that. You have to believe me."

"Was the car a bribe?"

Lauren set her coffee down, eyes wide. "Not exactly."

"What did they ask you to do?"

She sucked in a big breath. "I got an email. It said they wanted to talk about the case. I thought it was from the other attorney's office—I didn't know. I told them I couldn't meet in person because my car was in the shop." She lowered her voice. "Then this guy showed up after work – he was just there, waiting for me. He was really nice, and he said he knew I was Judge Henly's clerk."

"I don't understand," Annie said. "What did it matter? Why didn't they talk to the judge?"

Her shoulders dropped and she let out a breath. "Because everyone knows Judge Henly is old and waiting for retirement. My job is to research things for him, and most of the time he just agrees with whatever I come up with."

"I see," Annie said softly.

"But not always!" Lauren added. "The guy told me if I could make an argument against the fire department, he'd make it worth my while. I didn't think the judge would actually dismiss the case."

"I guess you were pretty convincing," Annie said.

"Annie, you have to believe me. I didn't think it would blow up like this. I didn't think it was a big deal. I honestly didn't think much of it at all."

Clearly.

Annie set her drink down and leaned forward. "How can you be sure this guy didn't have something to do with the fire?"

It was best not to tell Lauren she'd seen someone in the parking lot. Better to see what she would reveal.

"Why would they?"

"Because I was asking you questions about it at the fundraiser." Annie paused. "Did you tell them I was asking about it?"

Lauren shook her head vigorously. "No, absolutely not. After he dropped off the car, I never spoke to him again. I swear. They wouldn't have known you were figuring things out. Though now I'm sure everyone will put it together." She rubbed the back of her neck.

Annie couldn't say much on that front. Lauren and the judge would both come under a lot of scrutiny, though ultimately, it had been his call to dismiss the case, even if it was done out of laziness.

"So they don't have any suspects?" Lauren asked.

"They won't tell me anything," Annie said. "I just...I had to be sure. I had to talk to you about it."

Lauren sighed. "That's fair. I guess I'm a criminal."

"I didn't think you were a criminal," Annie said, chancing a smile. "But, come on, the Porsche is pretty glaring."

She groaned. "I didn't get to pick the car. I would've asked for a minivan."

"The dream," Annie said.

She decided now was not the right time to tell Lauren her own exciting news – Roy had offered to buy Annie a new car. Apparently the guilt associated with Annie almost dying in a fire had inspired more generosity in him.

"Do you hate me now?" Lauren asked, pulling Annie out of her thoughts.

Annie looked at her, surprise in her eyes. "No. I don't hate you."

"I didn't tell you this before," she shook her head, "I don't know why. But Roger lost his job and has been out of work for a year. It's been so stressful and I just wanted a car that was safe for the kids and..."

Tears flooded Lauren's eyes.

Annie felt her chest constrict. She couldn't condone what Lauren had done, but she could understand it.

She stood, arms outstretched. Lauren shot to her feet, dashing away a tear on her cheek, and took Annie into an embrace.

"I'm so sorry about everything," Lauren sobbed. "And I thank God you're okay."

Annie squeezed her tight. "Me too."

· · ·

Her next stop was Miles' house. It was time to come clean about all of it, and while she'd told Lauren she wouldn't rat her out to the police, she'd never said anything about the fire department. They deserved to know forces were working against them.

She parked at home and made the walk to his house. She wanted a moment to admire it before he noticed her, to listen to the birds chirping, the bees buzzing in his perfectly kept flowerbeds, and to admire the blue sky hanging overhead like a portrait of happiness.

The memory of him ripping her away from that fire flashed in her mind. The day she had almost died.

Whatever happened now, nothing could be as bad as that, even if her heart hadn't gotten the message, pounding away as if locked in a cage.

She knocked on the door. The sound of steps echoed, and then there he was, standing tall and handsome in a blue and black flannel shirt, the top button undone. His face was dark with stubble, more than his usual, and he had bags under his eyes.

"Annie."

The hard look was gone from his face, replaced with astonishment.

"Hi, Miles. Can I come in?"

"Of course."

He stepped aside and she walked in, pulling her coat off.

"I need to tell you something," she said.

The alarm on his face only grew, and he led her to the kitchen. He had a pot of tea brewed and poured a cup for each of them.

They sat at the kitchen table, and she told him everything about Lauren's car, her own suspicions, and finally the confrontation.

"Do you believe her?" Miles asked.

Annie considered this, watching the steam rise from her mug of tea. "I do. I think she did a dumb thing. But I don't think she's a murderer."

He nodded. "I'm not sure it matters. Everyone's up in arms about the judge dismissing the case, but what's done is done. We've moved on anyway. We might get some traction now with our new lawsuit."

Annie was surprised how little he cared about Lauren's actions – but he was right. They'd already accepted the loss and moved on.

"I'm glad to hear it." She stood.

He rushed to his feet. "Was there anything else? How are you doing?"

"I'm good." She paused. "I'm great, actually. But I won't take any more of your time."

"It's nice to see you. I'm glad you're – " He paused. "That you're well."

This was her chance. For once in her life, Annie wasn't going to overthink it. She wasn't going to think at all.

Before she'd come, she didn't know what she was going to say or do. She only knew she had to see Miles.

Now she was going on instinct. His handsome face was contorted with a politely puzzled expression, and his kind, soft eyes were focused on her. He stood broad-shouldered and tall, gazing down, his hands stuffed into his pockets, like he was holding himself back, like he hadn't swept her up.

Her hero. Her friend.

The man she would forever be desperately in love with.

"I've never properly thanked you." She stepped closer, breathing in his masculine cologne.

"Uh, you have nothing to – "

She didn't wait to hear his excuse again. Annie popped onto her tiptoes and planted her lips onto his.

He startled at first, but Annie kept kissing him, placing one hand on the back of his neck, her other hand around his back.

His muscles relaxed and he leaned into her, a gasp escaping his lips, a smile forming.

Then she broke the kiss, turned, and left.

Thirty

Warmth glowed on his skin, as though he'd just stepped out of the sun.

Miles stood in the doorway, mouth hanging open, until Annie was halfway down the street.

The sun was quickly disappearing.

His muscles tensed and he ran after her.

"Wait! Where are you going?" he yelled.

Annie turned, her big eyes looking up at him. "Home, I guess."

He blinked at her. "What was that?"

A smile lit her face, pink pooling into her cheeks. "I don't know. It just – happened."

"It just happened," he repeated.

A laugh burst from her and she clapped a hand to her mouth.

Miles laughed, too. It was astonishing. All this time he thought he was the only one fighting the irresistible urge to be closer to her. He thought he was being a gentleman by holding back – barely, sometimes, but at least attempting to.

But she had just up and kissed him like it was nothing.

"Nearly dying made me a little crazy," she said, clearing her throat. "So I'm sorry about that. I know I'm not what you're looking for. I hope it doesn't ruin our friend – "

He cut her off. "What makes you think you're not what I'm looking for?"

She swallowed. "I know you're dating that doctor, and I'm sorry if you two are exclusive and I just forced you to have to explain something to her." She looked down, as if this was just dawning on her for the first time. "Oh my gosh, I'm sorry. I really didn't think that far. I wasn't thinking at all."

A grin spread across his face. "What makes you think I'm seeing Dr. Birch?"

Her brows knit together. "I saw you together at the fundraiser. She was your date."

He shook his head, taking a step closer to her. "Not my date."

"Oh," she said, her eyes flicking up to him, then back down. "Well, I guess I got that wrong."

Though her boldness was failing under his questioning, it was the only spark he needed. Miles couldn't hold back any longer.

"I am not interested in her," he said slowly, stepping closer to her. "Because the only person I can think about, and the only person filling my head, is you."

Annie's lips parted. "What?"

What did she think would happen when she kissed him like that?

"Annie!" He laughed. "Is that so hard to believe?"

Her gray eyes glowed positively blue under the bright sky. "Sort of. Yes."

He took her hand into his. "I must be a much better actor than I realized, because I was sure you knew how I felt. I thought I was being a complete nuisance."

"A nuisance!" she repeated. "Miles, I..." she stammered, "I was desperately trying not to be one of those women who threw themselves at you, but I found that impossible not to do."

He grinned, pulling her in closer, placing her arm behind him. "Is that right?"

"Yes, much to my embarrassment," she went on, a smile dancing on her lips. "I find you as irresistible as the rest of the state."

"So you started the fire, then? To see if I'd save you?" he asked.

Her eyes narrowed. "We don't joke about fires, Miles."

He nodded solemnly. "We don't joke about fires."

Except he had to joke, or else the enormity of it would force him to his knees.

A lump formed in his throat. "I'm sorry if it seems like I've been avoiding you."

"I thought you were sick of me," Annie said.

"No, Annie. No." He shook his head before sucking in a deep breath. "I'm just a coward."

"No, you are not."

"I am. I thought I'd lost you that day. And the thought of losing you was so terrifying that, I don't know, I shut down."

She gazed up at him, her expression placid. "I'm sorry, Miles."

"I can't bear the thought of losing you, Annie. After Madeline, I didn't think I'd ever put myself together again. I managed to do it once, by some miracle, but I was determined to never fall in love again." He paused. "Then I met you, and I think I've been in love with you from the first day I saw you."

"Oh?" She laughed, a little breathlessly. "You don't remember the grocery store, do you?"

He cocked his head to the side. "The grocery store?"

She waved a hand. "Never mind. I'll tell you when you're older."

Miles stared at her, his mind unable to catch up to everything that was happening.

She meant it all, didn't she? She'd meant the kiss. She didn't think he was a nuisance. She'd even said something about throwing herself at him.

And he meant it, too. "I can't bear the thought of losing you. I really can't."

"Then don't," she said simply.

His chest went from a sun-kissed heat to a burning fire. There was no resisting her any longer. He pulled her in, pressing his lips to hers, his hands grasping at her, desperate to claim the curves he'd so longed to touch.

• • •

News of their union spread quickly. It was impossible to prevent, as Bella came home and spotted them walking down the street, holding hands.

Bella ran toward them, screaming, "Yes! I knew it! I *knew* it!"

Later that evening, over dinner at Annie's, Clara had a similarly contented reaction.

"I could see there was something between the two of you, but I figured it best to keep it to myself as to not scare you off."

"For once, Mom, you didn't say anything to Miles that embarrassed me!" Annie said.

She laughed. "That's right. Margie once tried to set Miles up and he'd scared her so badly she never forgot it."

Miles sat back, a laugh bursting out of him. "What? I don't remember that."

"Oh yes," Clara said. "You scared off a notorious matchmaker. Sheila, too, was certain you were off-limits. But Patty and I knew there was a chance."

He cleared his throat and looked down at his plate. "I didn't realize I was the talk of the town."

"Of course you were," Annie said. "With those pictures on the ferry? How could you not be?"

"You're welcome, Dad." Bella grinned. "He thinks he knows everything, but clearly, he doesn't."

"Thank goodness I have a teenage daughter who actually does know everything," he said dryly.

She stuck out her tongue at him and the table erupted in giddy laughter.

The next weekend, Miles took Annie on their first proper date.

Miles, who had been riding a high for the entirety of the week, needed to knock it out of the park.

This was the woman he'd been pining after for months. A woman of incredible beauty, strength, and wisdom. Their first date couldn't be dinner and a movie. It had to at least attempt to live up to her.

He asked Bella to babysit the kids. She was thrilled, already referring to them as her baby brother and sister. She and Clara decided to hang out after the kids were asleep and watch a movie; Bella had yet to inform her that she was her new grandma, but Miles was sure it was coming.

For the evening, he booked a sunset cruise with a private chef. He dressed in a suit and picked Annie up at the door, presenting her with a bouquet of three dozen roses.

"I can't imagine what you have planned," she said as they walked to the car. She was delighted when they got to the marina and spotted the boat.

"Is this the same one from the auction?"

"It is," he said with a nod, offering his arm for the walk down the dock.

"Well, Mr. Coleman," she said, "you've truly outdone yourself. And outspent yourself! What were you thinking?"

"I'm thinking I've gotten a date with the most beautiful woman on earth and I am not going to mess it up."

She looked down, smiling, before turning to him. "You could never mess it up."

Except then, as they settled into their seats, the captain appeared to tell them that the engine wouldn't start and they were stuck for the evening.

"I still think it's very romantic," Annie said.

The candlelight flickered between them, casting a warm glow on her exquisite face. Those eyes, those lips, everything about her was perfection.

"The whole thing's a disaster," he grumbled, sitting back. "I want the best for you, Annie."

"You're going to have to let go of that." The side of her mouth tilted. "Besides, the best for me is...you."

His face cracked into a smile and within seconds, he was on his knees next to her, kissing her hands. "Yeah, well. I'll take any disaster, as long as I get to be with you."

"Works for me."

She tilted her head down and he raised himself to meet her kiss.

Epilogue

On a blooming Saturday in June, Sheila and Russell wed. The day could not have been any more magnificent. Annie stared at the blue sky as she got out of her car. It was the perfect weather for the knee-length yellow dress she'd picked for the occasion.

When Miles had picked her and the twins up for the short trip to the church, he mimed his heart jumping from his chest.

"You look like the sun," he said.

Annie looked down at herself. "Sweaty and cancer-causing?"

He didn't miss a beat. "The center of everything."

He looked impossibly broad and handsome in his navy blue suit. She had to fight the urge to leap into his arms and smother his face in kisses when she first saw him, settling instead for a kiss on the cheek.

The twins spun around her, chasing one another and yelling in the church parking lot. She narrowly rescued Noel from splashing into a murky puddle as Miles swept a whining Leon into his arms.

"Got you!" he said.

"No!" Leon raised a hand to deliver a slap, but Miles promptly blew a raspberry into his arm and sent him into giggles.

Sheila had asked if Leon and Noel wanted to be the ring bearer and flower girl. Noel was thrilled, practicing with baskets of fake flower petals at home, but Leon declined to participate after seeing several example videos of what his duties would be.

His talking had wildly improved. He'd graduated from speech therapy, so Annie knew he meant what he said. When they got into the church and joined the hurried rush of the wedding party, Annie left to prepare to coach Noel down the aisle, while Leon went off happily with Miles and Bella.

They stood in the back, greeting the arriving guests who gushed over Noel's adorable white dress and floral headband. Noel relished the attention, smiling her biggest smile and clutching her flower basket with tiny hands.

As much as it wasn't Leon's scene, it certainly was Noel's, and she basked in every moment. Annie thought her heart might burst from cuteness.

Sheila was hidden away, but her impressive fleet of brides-maids appeared and whisked them into a side room. Included were Sheila's daughters Eliza, Mackenzie, Shelby, and Emma; Russell's daughter Mia; and Sheila's sisters Addy and Kara.

Russell had an equally impressive wall of groomsmen at his side at the end of the aisle: his son, Lucas; Jacob, Mia's boyfriend and Annie's longtime friend; Joey, Russell's private pilot and Eliza's beau; and Rick, Addy's boyfriend. There were three other men Annie wasn't familiar with, but judging from their absurdly handsome faces, they were probably fellow movie stars.

Five minutes before they were set to begin, Sheila entered the room. Annie gasped. She wore a silk organza gown in ivory, with a high neck and cascading ruffles running down the dress, giving a romantic, petal-like effect. Her hair was pulled back in a loose braid, a white flower behind her ear.

"You look like a dream!" Annie said.

Sheila grinned, a glint in her eye. "Thank you, Annie. How about we get this show on the road before we start losing people?"

"You got it." Annie nodded, leaving Noel in Margie's care for a brief moment, quietly slipping to the front of the church. Leon spotted her immediately, a grin spreading on his face as he waved. She waved back, unable to contain her smile.

The music began and Noel started her march, her expression serious, throwing petals forward, backward, and adding flourishes until she reached the front.

"That was wonderful," Annie whispered before whisking her to their seats next to Miles, Bella, and Leon.

Russell stood tall, tears in his eyes as the bridesmaids made their way down the aisle, holding bouquets overflowing with peonies and wildflowers.

The bridal march rang out, and they rose to their feet. Sheila appeared, grinning and eyes brimming with tears, with Patty at her side to give her away.

That was all it took. Annie wasn't particularly good at keeping her own tears in at weddings, but this time she started her weeping early, before Sheila had even made it to her groom.

Miles leaned in, planting a kiss on her cheek and squeezing her hand. Annie squeezed his hand back, but she couldn't chance looking at him at the risk of completely losing it.

Once seated, Annie recovered some semblance of control. Patty's golden retriever Derby served as ring bearer, and he barreled down the aisle, stopping and sprinting, soliciting back scratches from obliging guests and causing outbursts of laughter.

When they said their vows, Annie's tears returned, streaming down her face. Her heart was overfilled with happiness, and gratitude, and joy. She had been so endlessly, blissfully happy these past months.

She could hardly believe it was real. Miles was an absurdly attentive boyfriend, helping with daycare pickups, making dinners, and surprising her at work with flowers or coffee – anything for an excuse to see her. Bella was more than thrilled by their relationship, insisting on babysitting the twins, whom she referred to exclusively as "my baby brother and sister."

With Roy's new payments, Annie was able to move out of her mom's place and into a rental house one street over. It gave them a bit of breathing room without taking them too far from her mom or Miles.

Still, it ruined Miles' plan. "I wanted to lure you into marrying me by offering my big, empty house for your liking."

Annie grinned at him. "There will be time for that."

There was no need to rush. She had no doubt they would have the rest of their lives together.

Once Sheila and Russell sprinted down the aisle and out of the church, Annie could finally stop crying. The mass of people, which included surprisingly fewer celebrities than expected, made their way to Saltwater Cove for the reception.

Margie had pulled out all the stops: fresh flowers everywhere the eye could see, their sweet fragrance in the air. Craft cocktails awaited the guests as they walked in, and waiters passed endless hors d'oeuvres of Dungeness crab, smoked salmon crostini, and seared scallops. Inside the barn, the tables were set with crisp white linen, gold flatware, and gold chairs. The walls were draped in floor to ceiling satin, and in the center stood a glittering champagne tower.

The bride and groom arrived by seaplane, laughing as they wobbled onto the dock to their cheering guests. They proceeded to the outdoor dance floor for their first dance, the live band playing *Head over Heels* by Tears for Fears.

Annie stood at the edge of the dance floor, trying to hold Noel and Leon back, when Sheila's mother Marilyn approached.

"Wouldn't be my choice for a first dance song," she said glumly. "But I suppose Sheila likes the song after Russell serenaded her with it."

She was dressed in a white, floor-length gown. Annie suppressed a smile. "I think it's romantic."

"You know," Marilyn added, "I'd suggested to Sheila I would've made a great flower girl, but she decided to go with your little one instead."

Miles opened his mouth to respond, but Annie held up a hand. She was all too familiar with Sheila's mother through Eliza.

"The flower-grandma is very chic," Annie said brightly. "Maybe you'll get your chance with Eliza."

A smile spread across her face. "Maybe I will!"

The evening was filled with more magic – a fleet of food trucks, marshmallow toasting on fire department approved gas fireplaces, and portrait artists painting the guests.

Annie disappeared for an hour to put the kids to bed, and Clara volunteered to stay with them so she could return to the party.

Miles, of course, went with her. He took the responsibility of keeping her safe very seriously, hardly ever leaving her side.

It wasn't totally necessary. A month after the fire, Chief Hank arrested Alex. He crumbled quickly, saying he had no idea Annie had been inside the building. He'd wanted to send a message and asked for leniency because he was the one who had initially called the fire in once he'd realized his mistake.

With Alex in jail, there was no other danger to her, but Annie didn't care what excuse Miles used. She loved every minute with him. He made every aspect of life easier. It wasn't just that he added to her life; he verifiably completed it. It felt like she'd been waiting for him all this time.

The quiet moments with him, steady at her side, made her grateful for everything she'd gone through in the last year – with Roy, the fire, everything. It had led her to Miles, and she wouldn't change a single thing.

As the sun set, Margie called Sheila, Russell and their guests to the shore. The sky burned orange and red, and against the stunning backdrop, a white boat appeared in the distance.

From inside, Lottie's trainers waved. Sheila and Russell looked at each other, accusation in their eyes.

"My idea," Mackenzie confessed, beaming.

Moments later, a black fin broke the water. Lottie broke the surface, blowing a breath nearby.

The crowd cheered, and once again, Annie fought back tears. She knew Lottie was still taken for "walks," but she had never expected this. Apparently, neither had Sheila or Russell, the two of them clinging to each other and staring in wonder.

Lottie disappeared, and it was so quiet that all they could hear was the gentle sound of water at the rocky shore.

Then Lottie exploded from beneath the surface, slamming into the water with a cascading splash. The guests erupted into cheers again, and Lottie, apparently reverting to her old training, leapt from the water repeatedly, splashing and celebrating.

Miles pulled a tissue from his pocket and handed it to Annie. She wiped away the tears, then stood, leaning her back against Miles' broad chest.

She could never have imagined how wonderful life could be. She could never have imagined this.

Annie closed her eyes, memorizing the moment.

Reader's Newsletter

Want to dive deeper into the Spotted Cottage Series?

Sign up to Amelia's newsletter and get bonus content from the entire Spotted Cottage series including:

- Rick's postcard to Addy
- Recipes from Eliza and Patty
- A bonus chapter with Sheila and Russell's first Christmas

Visit https://mailchi.mp/0548bfa882d1/rick to get your copy now!

About the Author

Amelia Addler writes always sweet, always swoon-worthy romance stories and believes that everyone deserves their own happily ever after.

Her soulmate is a man who once spent five weeks driving her to work at 4AM after her car broke down (and he didn't complain, not even once). She is lucky enough to be married to that man and they live in Pittsburgh with their little yellow mutt. Visit her website at AmeliaAddler.com or drop her an email at amelia@AmeliaAddler.com.

Also by Amelia...

The Spotted Cottage Series
The Spotted Cottage by the Sea
A Spot of Tea
A Spot at Starlight Beach
Spotted at Lighthouse Bay
A Spot of Summer
A Spot of Grace

The Westcott Bay Series
Saltwater Cove
Saltwater Studios
Saltwater Secrets
Saltwater Crossing
Saltwater Falls
Saltwater Memories
Saltwater Promises

The Orcas Island Series
Sunset Cove
Sunset Secrets
Sunset Tides
Sunset Weddings
Sunset Serenade